Kissing Charlie

Elsa Winckler

The characters and events in this book are fictitious. Any similarity to real persons, living or dead, places, or events is coincidental and not intended by the author.

ISBN: (ebook) 978-1-953335-67-8
(print) 978-1-953335-68-5

Inkspell Publishing
207 Moonglow Circle #101
Murrells Inlet, SC 29576

Edited By Rie Langdon
Cover Art By Fantasia Frog

DEDICATION

To everyone struggling to adapt to our 'new normal'.

CHAPTER 1

Charlie finally focused on the gray, knotted tie. Nobody in the small town of Alisson, Montana, population seven thousand, wore a tie and even if, on the very odd occasion, they did, it didn't look like this one. Precisely and perfectly done, like the rest of the man in front of her.

She should probably try breathing again. Now she understood Lilly's giggle when she'd announced Charlie's new client.

The minute he'd entered her consulting room, something sucked all the oxygen from the room in a matter of seconds, leaving her breathless.

Valiantly, she'd tried to inhale, but around them, the air was vibrating with strange undercurrents.

"There must be a mistake," the man said, "I'm looking for…" He glanced at his phone. "Charlie Wilson?"

She finally managed to get some air in her lungs. "I am Charlene Wilson, Charlie to my friends. How can I help you?" Nearly cringing, she held out her hand. Where did the sudden husky voice come from? She didn't usually sound like this.

For a moment, he stared at her outstretched hand before he took his out of his pocket and extended it

1

forward. Fascinated, she stared as his hand folded around hers. Fingers touched, and...wow. An electric shock literally sent shivers down her spine. Shivers? Trying her best to swallow the hysterical giggle threatening to escape, she quickly dropped her hand. She was twenty-eight, for crying out loud; behaving like a schoolgirl was so not the thing to do right now.

Granted, the guy was drop-dead gorgeous. Broad shoulders, light brown hair slicked back, not one strand out of place—probably didn't dare—square jaw, brilliant blue eyes; his entire presence emanated an air of purpose and authority. Clearly a man who liked to have everything under control.

Impatiently, he glanced around him. "I'm Logan Johnson. My mother, Eleanor, made an appointment for me."

Of course, her lunch appointment was with Eleanor's son. She'd known that, but she'd completely forgotten about that little detail for a moment. Eleanor often spoke about her "beautiful son in Seattle," but beautiful didn't begin to describe the man in front of her.

Before Charlie could answer, he rubbed his face, clearly exasperated. "But I thought it was with a medical professional and a...well, not..." He pointed toward the words on her door. "A 'Bowen therapist,' whatever the hell that means. I don't know what she was thinking. Sorry to have wasted your time." He turned around to leave and in that instant, she noticed the way he stiffly held the upper part of his body.

Damn it, it was her job to look for signs like this when her clients entered her room, but she'd been so occupied perving about the gorgeous specimen of a man, she hadn't noticed the usual telltale clues of someone in pain.

She relaxed. He was clearly upset because one, he'd thought she was a man, and two, he wasn't comfortable with what she did. But it was also obvious he needed help, and that, she could provide.

"Chicken?" she asked his retreating back.

He stopped and slowly turned around. "Excuse me?"

"You're in pain. I can help you. The only reason why you won't let me try is either because I'm a woman or because you're afraid."

His eyes narrowed. "I am certainly not afraid. But I am not prepared to let some"—he motioned in the air with his hands—"pseudo-whatever, put his or her hands on me. I'm in enough pain as it is. What the hell does 'Bowen therapist' mean, anyway?" Before she could answer, he sniffed in the air. "And I smell lavender and something woody—what is it?"

Charlie lifted her chin and squared her shoulders. "My sister, Lindsay, and I are both trained nurses. Medical professionals. She has the shop adjacent to my rooms, selling essential oils—that's what you're smelling—and I'm trained as a Bowen technique therapist. The Bowen technique is well known in the medical profession and if you give me a chance, I promise you I can help."

He moved as if to turn, and winced. Grabbing on to the back of the chair with one hand, he cursed under his breath.

Interesting. Not so in control all the time, apparently.

"I can help you," she repeated, holding her breath. It would be better it if he'd simply leave. The mere thought of having to put her hands on him had her all flustered. But however unpleasant and uptight he was, she'd have to try and help him; otherwise, she'd worry about him all day.

Fortunately, Bowen Therapy did not require intense massaging; surely she could do this without having palpitations, for goodness' sake.

He finally spoke. "Okay, damn it, I'm here. Let's do this. But if you do any hocus-pocus stuff, I'm out of here."

Her hands were itching to pick up something to throw at him, but pressing her lips together to make sure she wouldn't say anything she'd regret later, she pointed toward the table.

"Please lie down on your back." She pulled the curtain around the padded table. "There is no need for you to take off your clothes…" Images of his naked body nearly had her tripping over her own feet. "But you may be more comfortable without your jacket and…and tie."

She waited until he'd disappeared behind the curtain before she exhaled. What was wrong with her, for goodness' sake? Here she was, nearly hyperventilating, and all because of a man. Yes, he was seriously attractive, but he was, nevertheless, just a man.

One with a perfectly knotted tie.

He was lying down, as she'd instructed, when she opened the curtain.

"How did you hurt your back?" Her voice was cool, and she wasn't meeting his eyes.

"While hiking," he said curtly. He was in pain; it didn't matter what the hell happened. "Tell me about this Wowen, Bowen, whatever the hell you call this cr— therapy."

She gave him a cool look. "It's called Bowen Therapy."

"Bowen Therapy," he said, his gaze on her mouth.

"The guiding principles of the technique were established by Tom Bowen during the 1950s. It focuses on the whole person, not just the condition. In other words, it treats the cause, not only the symptoms. It helps the body to heal and restores the balance by shifting the body from your innate 'fight or flight' system to a more natural state of calm."

He watched her as she studied his body. She was holding something in her hand. Damn, she had yet to touch him, but he was struggling not to react to her nearness. The fact that he was lying on his back wasn't helping, either.

"Natural state of calm? With you doing strange things to my body?" he grumbled, only realizing the ambiguity of his words when they hung in the air around them.

4

Her lips twitched.

"Oh, you think this is funny?" he snarled.

"I think you're in pain. I think you like being in control and at the moment, you're not. That's why you feel the need to lash out. But it's fine. I often have children throwing tantrums."

"I'm not throwing a tantrum, damn it…" He tried to sit up straight, but a pain shot up his back, and groaning, he had to slowly lie down again.

"The movements in Bowen Therapy," she continued as if he hadn't interrupted her, "are very distinctive and are used on precise points on the body. It involves moving the soft tissue in a particular way. I will use a rolling-type movement, using my fingers, hands, or sometimes my elbow. It will create a focus for the brain by stimulating the nerve pathways and tissue. I work on only a small area, depending how far your skin can move. What you may find strange—"

"This whole damn day is strange. I don't know what the hell my mother was thinking," he muttered.

But the lady was not to be fazed. "—is that in between working on you, I'll leave the room. This is when the body starts repairing itself. Close your eyes, please?"

Close his eyes? Not while he had no idea what she was going to do. And how the hell could anything be repaired when she'd be leaving the damn room? This would teach him not to ever listen to his mother again.

"Please?" she asked, and smiled.

He closed his eyes quickly. If he had to look at her for one more minute, he'd be in trouble. It was getting more and more difficult to keep his body under control as it was.

"Okay, keep your eyes closed and breathe," she crooned, after a few seconds. Bangles jingled, soft hands touched his sides, moved slowly toward his back. To the exact spot where the pain was. His eyes flew open.

"How do know…?"

"I used a crystal," she muttered. She was bending over

him, her earrings—miniature chandeliers, really—were caressing her cheek and her long hair fell forward like a curtain, touching his shirt. Roses. That was what he was smelling. His body reacted and he swallowed a groan. The woman was killing him.

He couldn't remember the last time he'd had such a physical reaction to someone he'd just met.

She lifted her arms and moved away. "I'm going out of the room now. Close your eyes and try to…relax." The last word was muffled as she quickly left the room.

Damn it to hell and back. He should've paid more attention when she'd phoned to sing the praises of the "wonderful therapist" Charlie, who, she'd claimed, had "fixed" her neck, leaving her free of pain for the first time in years. She hadn't mentioned that "Charlie" was a gorgeous-looking woman.

He should've remembered his mother never did anything normal people did.

But she'd phoned when he'd been on his way to a meeting he was already late for. He'd eventually caved, partly because the meeting had been about to begin and partly because he'd felt so guilty he hadn't been back home since his sister Brooke's husband's funeral two years before.

It wasn't as if he hadn't seen his family, though. His mom, Brooke, and her son, Connor, had visited him in Seattle a few times over the last two years, and they'd all been to his cabin in Mount Rainier National Park near the city a couple of times.

There wasn't really time in his busy schedule to fly to Bozeman, get a car, and then still drive the extra forty minutes to Alisson. He was the CEO of a fund-managing company and worked twenty-four-seven. It had been his goal in life to make enough money so that he could have the life he wanted.

But, he'd calculated, this way he'd manage to see his mom and sister and maybe get some relief from the constant backache that had been plaguing him for the last few weeks. Time in his busy day to find out where a good physio or chiropractor was, he didn't have. Anna, his PA, would gladly help, but this was the kind of thing he'd rather do himself. Nobody else needed to know how much pain he was in.

What he hadn't expected, though, was that the "therapist" would be so beautiful. He saw pretty women every day, but something about this therapist had caught him off guard. With clear blue eyes, long, blond curls cascading down her back, and a slim body, she was simply exquisite.

But what the hell was she wearing? In a glittering pink top that left her arms bare while delicate lace gathered gently around her long neck, and a soft, layered skirt that fell to the ground, she didn't look like any medical professional he knew.

The women he was used to, and whom he met on a daily basis in business, wore appropriate suits that didn't distract from the work at hand. And he'd been on his way out of the door of Charlie's office—he still wasn't sure how he'd ended up on this table, on his back. Yet here he was, trusting someone he didn't know from Adam to relieve his pain.

Why on earth would his mother think he would let a…a…gypsy like this treat his back?

Charlie braced herself before she opened the door to her office again. Fortunately, Lindsay and Lilly were still out to lunch because otherwise they both would've noticed Charlie's flushed face when she'd literally fled her own rooms a few minutes ago. She had no idea how to explain what was happening.

He'd reacted to her—she couldn't help but notice it. What she hadn't expected, though, was what the sight of his "reaction" did to her. In her tight top, her hardened nipples were easily noticeable; she'd had to get out of there quickly. Hopefully, the ridiculous moment had passed and she'd return to her cool self.

Still muttering, she opened the door. Logan was sitting on the table.

"You're not supposed to move," she scolded. "But since you're up…" Her gaze flew to his crotch before she could help it and her ability to speak disappeared.

"So, you've noticed." His jaw was stiff, his eyes mere slits. I'm…sorry, and—"

She cut him off with a wave of jingling bangles and cleared her throat. "Please lie on your stomach." He was undoubtedly embarrassed because his body was refusing to toe the line.

Oh, my word, what's up with the husky voice today?

Scowling, he lay down with a grunt and she put her hands on his back.

"What are you doing now?"

"Just relax." While applying subtle, relaxing rolling moves across the muscles and tendons of his lower back, she tried her best not to look at his broad shoulders, his narrow hips, his perfectly rounded butt.

This was going to be the longest forty-five minutes of her life.

It was only after he'd put on his jacket that it hit him: his mother was trying to set him up with the lovely therapist.

He'd been wracking his brain, trying to understand why his mother would send him to someone like Charlie Wilson. He'd been here for what felt like an eternity, but he was still in pain. What the hell the "technique" was, he still had no idea, but she'd barely touched his body. A few feather-like movements would be followed by her leaving the room, and each damn time he was left aching for more of her touch. This was no real therapy.

He cursed under his breath. Whatever she was doing, it was obviously utter nonsense and if his body hadn't been so out of control, he would've caught on much earlier.

But now his brain cells had finally started working again, and it was clear as daylight what was going on here. His mother had figured he would fall for the lovely therapist, or whatever the hell she was, the minute he saw her.

He should have suspected something like this—his mother had been way too insistent. She wanted to see him married and settled. She wanted grandbabies, he was told regularly. But he never imagined she'd try and do something like this.

Just then the door opened and Charlie was back. And just as quickly, his body reacted to her again. With her nearby, there was no possibility of his body reaching a state of calm, as she'd so quaintly put it.

Fed up with the way his mother had conned him again, he tried counting silently to ten before he spoke, but he was still furious. "I've finally realized what's going on here. You're obviously in on the deal. So let me be perfectly clear—I'm not in the market for a wife. So this whole"—angrily, he motioned with his hand—"charade, was all in vain."

Her eyes widened and she caught her breath before she burst out laughing. Stunned, he could only stare. She laughed with utter abandon. Her whole body took part—blue eyes twinkled, the bangles on her arms jingled, even her hair was bouncing merrily to the sound.

He gnashed his teeth. "It's not funny."

She let out another giggle before she finally managed to gulp in her laugh. But her eyes were still filled with mirth. "I assure you, sir, getting married is so not something I'm interested in. I'm very happy with my life. You don't have to worry that I have designs…" Another giggle erupted before she quickly composed her face. "Drink lots of water when you get home and don't do any other strenuous exercises. And do give my best to your mother. She is a such lovely person."

He didn't miss the slight emphasis on "she." As Charlie spoke, she walked toward the door and opened it widely.

And that should have been that. He should have walked out, gotten into his car, and driven away.

Instead, his feet moved purposefully toward her. Again, her eyes widened, but this time it was in alarm.

"What are you doing?" she asked warily.

"I have no idea," he said, getting the words out somehow before he bent his head. The smell of roses hit him again, seeped through his skin, and heated his blood. His lips simply had to test the texture of her skin. For a millisecond, his mouth touched her temple. Petals. Satin. Soft.

"I wasn't the only one who was aroused," he muttered.

"Don't…" Her voice was a mere whisper.

Hastily, he stepped back. What the hell was wrong with him? Without saying another word, he stormed out. At this moment, he could cheerily throttle his mother.

CHAPTER 2

Charlie was still standing with her hand on the doorknob, utterly bemused, when Lindsay returned from lunch. Inside were sounds indicating that Lilly, the young girl they'd hired to help them, had also returned.

"It is just the most glorious summer's day outside. You should really take a walk. I love this time of year!" Lindsay sang, twirling around the office. Only when she caught sight of Charlie's face did her smile fade. "What's wrong?"

Charlie quickly moved forward and touched her sister's hand. Lindsay was so much better since they'd made the move from South Africa to this lovely town two years before; she didn't want to do or say anything that might upset her sister in any way.

"Nothing is wrong, sweetie, relax. I've just had a difficult client. You know, one of those who doesn't think what we do is 'professional.'"

"But weren't you supposed to see Eleanor's son over lunch? Don't tell me he is the difficult client? Both Eleanor and her daughter are so sweet."

"I know, right? I also find it hard to believe he's related to such lovely free spirits as Eleanor and Brooke. You should see him—my fingers literally itched to mess up his

11

hair and loosen his tie."

Lindsay's eyes widened in mock disbelief. "Mess up his hair? Loosen his tie? You seriously want to tell me my I'm-not-interested-in-men-period sister wants to actually touch a man? I have to see this guy!"

"Don't be ridiculous, of course I don't actually want to…to…" And suddenly the gentle pressure of warm lips against her temple replayed so vividly in her mind, she had to rub the place where his lips had been.

"Charlie?" Lindsay's voice finally penetrated her thoughts. "Your eyes kind of glazed over there for a minute—care to tell me why?"

Fortunately, Lilly called over to Lindsay; there was a client in the shop asking for her, and Charlie didn't have to answer.

"Don't think you're going to get away with it, it's Friday night. Tonight, I'll ply you with drinks until you confess." Lindsay grinned as she walked in the direction of the little shop adjacent to Charlie's rooms. "By the way," she asked over her shoulder, "is there now a final date for your meeting in Seattle?"

"Yes, the second Friday in July—in about three weeks' time. Why? You want to join me?"

"I've been thinking about it. There are quite a few companies selling essential oils in Seattle; it'll be nice to try to see at least one of them."

"Oh, Linds, that'll be so nice. We haven't been anywhere else since we arrived in Montana, and apparently Seattle is a beautiful city."

"Great—I'll check out flights and accommodation?"

Lilly appeared with Charlie's next client. "Thanks." She nodded to Lindsay before her sister slipped into her office.

Charlie greeted her client, but Lilly hovered. "So, tell me about the hot guy you saw earlier?" she whispered.

"Don't you have work?" Charlie asked Lilly.

"Mmmm, this is serious." Lilly giggled but before Charlie could say something, she left, waving her hand.

"I'm going, I'm going!"

Charlie groaned. Lindsay was bad, but Lilly was worse. They were going to pester her until they had all the details and some juicy tidbits.

But apart from the fact that Logan Johnson was rude and a snob, there really wasn't much else to tell anyone. Except to mention his very blue eyes, his broad shoulders, square jawline...

Exasperated with herself, she rubbed her face. She'd never had such a physical reaction to any man before. So why had she reacted like a sex-starved old maid? Okay, he was seriously attractive, but so were many other men. And it's not as if she didn't date or have sex. It had been a while, but she wasn't sex-starved, for goodness' sake.

But hopefully, this craziness would pass because she knew she could never get serious about anyone. Being dumped by her last boyfriend, Toby, because she couldn't have children, had kinda driven home the fact that she wasn't "marrying material," as he'd nastily put it.

It had taken her a while to come to grips with her reality, but after nearly four years, she'd learned to let go of the picture she'd always had in her head of a loving husband, a couple of kids, and a ranch. Maybe she'd be able to have a ranch one day, but she could never have children, and day by day she was learning to live with that particular heartache.

What irritated her most about herself was that only after Toby had left did she realize how much she'd gone out of her way to try and make him happy, and if he hadn't dumped her, she probably would still be jumping through hoops, trying to be the kind of woman he wanted.

From watching the way her friends made themselves smaller to keep the men in their lives happy, she could honestly say being in another relationship didn't look all that appealing.

And after Lindsay's experience with her last boyfriend, she'd let go of the idea of ever finding a loving husband.

It had taken her a while to discover who she really was, to dress to please herself and not a man, to do what made her happy and to live her life according to her rules and not someone else's.

Men, as this one had just proven again, loved to be in control. And she could control her own life quite effectively, thank you very much. She certainly didn't need a man to tell her how to behave.

And right now, her goal was to make a home for herself and Lindsay and to provide a calm and stable environment for her sister. Both of them had been lost after their parents' sudden deaths. That period of turmoil, of grief, was probably the reason why Lindsay had fallen for the first guy she thought could give her stability. And Charlie had been so busy feeling sorry for herself, she hadn't noticed the signs in time to warn her sister. And so Lindsay had ended up in a nightmare.

She put her hand on her heart. It was still racing like a runaway train. Aaargh, she was simply going to ignore this spark or jolt or whatever one called this craziness.

Fortunately, she wouldn't see him again.

But as she walked back into her rooms where her next client was waiting, her hand strayed up to her temple again. Oh, my goodness, this was ridiculous. She had work to do; she didn't drool over men.

Logan's mother was looking perplexed. "I don't think I follow you. You're unhappy because you don't think Charlie looked the right part?"

"No… Yes! And you deliberately let me believe Charlie is a man!"

"Since when does that make a difference?" his mother asked.

His sister, who had just popped in from her house next door, also had something to add. "I can just picture the scene. You all superior and haughty, telling her she wasn't dressed according to Logan Johnson's rules. How can I ever go back to Charlie and Lindsay? And they're the best!"

"Mom, you were trying to set me up with her—don't even try to deny it!" he bellowed.

Both of them fell silent for a moment before they burst out laughing.

Brooke was the first one to recover. "Set you up with Charlie? Mom will certainly never set up the lovely Charlie with someone as...as... Come on, Mom, help me. Describe your son."

His mom finally stopped laughing. "My dear child," she said and cupped his face for a moment, "I love you to bits, as you know, but you're simply too...too ..." She looked at Brooke. "What is the right word?"

He scowled at his mom and sister. "Seriously? So, I'm the problem?"

Grinning, Brooke snapped her fingers. "Boring, Mom. Describes my brother to a tee."

His mother nodded. Nodded! "Too boring for Charlie, in any case. The two of you would've made beautiful babies, but alas, no, sweetheart. You, my dear boy, are too predictable, too rigid, too controlling for someone like our Charlie. You're too much like a...like a..."

"Man?" Brooke offered.

"I am a man, damn it!" he snapped, highly irritated.

"What I mean," his mom said, "is Charlie needs someone who will get her, you know? And let's face it, son, you prefer your women rake-thin, groomed within an inch of their life, and without any personality. And that"— grinning, she shook her head—"is not Charlie. Don't you just love the way she dresses? It's so rare to see a woman embracing who she is and dressing accordingly, without trying to please anyone else."

"The way she dresses? Mom, she looks... I don't even know how to describe her style. If you can even call it style."

His mom's eyes lit up. "It's called Boho, and isn't it fabulous?"

"Mom," Brooke said and glanced at her watch. "If you want to change before we leave, you should hurry up, it's getting late."

"Go where?" Logan asked.

"Over weekends, we meet up with our friends in one of the local bars-slash-breweries. Everybody seems to be brewing beer these days, even in Alisson," his mother said. "But don't worry, I know it's not your scene. I've made something for you to eat so you can go to bed early."

Clair moved toward the front door. "Okay, Mom, I'm going to change. The babysitter is already with Connor; I'll just get my bag. Ten minutes?"

"You realize I've come to visit you for the weekend?" he asked crossly.

His mother rubbed his arm. "Of course, but you told me how tired you were, and I thought you'd like to go to bed early tonight."

"Not at half past six!"

"Well," Brooke said from the door, "Friday nights, Mom and I go out. You're welcome to join us, but that means you'll have to lose the tie, and that'll make you so unhappy," she teased, before closing the door behind her, still giggling.

"Just relax and try not to work tonight," his mom said.

"Damn it, I don't want to go to bed!" he scowled. "I'll come with you," he muttered and walked toward his room. Spending the night at the local bar sounded infinitely better than sitting here and replaying scenes of his lips on Charlie Wilson's temple.

They'd called him boring. He wasn't boring; his workday was filled with exciting things happening all the time. The volatile financial market could never be called boring. Okay, yes, he liked neat and tidy women who knew he wasn't interested in anything long-term, but that wasn't boring. Was it?

A few drinks would also help him sleep better. His back was still killing him and on top of that, another part of his body was also still misbehaving.

Cursing under his breath, he looked around the room where he'd be staying. "Neat and tidy" weren't concepts either his mother or his sister understood. Both were well-known and respected artists and both seemed to thrive in chaos.

It was obvious his mother had made an effort to clear out this room, but there was so much stuff, it seemed she'd given up halfway through the process.

Still cursing a blue streak, he opened his overnight bag. This was why he preferred his own space. The bag was exactly as he liked it—uncluttered, neat, tidy with nothing unnecessary lying around.

He still vividly remembered the way his whole world had fallen into disarray after his father had died. His dad had been the one who'd kept things together, and after he had gone, it seemed his mom simply gave up trying to keep things in order.

Tomorrow he'd spend time with Connor before he'd find an excuse to head back to Seattle. This clutter was driving him insane.

Roses. Why was he smelling roses? For the first time, he noticed the small vase his mother had filled with roses. Without really thinking about it, he picked it up and sniffed the delicate petals. And immediately he was back in Charlie's rooms that afternoon, his mouth trailing a path over her satiny skin…

"Logan?" his mom called from downstairs.

He put the vase down quickly. What the hell was wrong with him, daydreaming about a woman he'd just met?

His mother was waiting for him at the bottom of the stairs. The twinkle in her eyes stopped him. Exasperated, he gave her a hug. "You've conned me into going with you tonight, haven't you?"

She laughed. "I don't know what you're talking about.

Shall we take your car?"

"Yeah, right," he said, but couldn't help the grin. His mom was something else.

CHAPTER 3

"Oh, look," exclaimed Lindsay, pointing toward the entrance to the pub. "It's Brooke and her mother." Her eyes widened. "And if I'm not mistaken, Eleanor's son is with them. No tie, though." She giggled and waved.

"Lindsay, no!" Charlie hissed, but Lindsay was already calling out to them. Charlie was sitting with her back toward the door, so she had a few minutes to try and compose herself before the Johnson family reached their table.

"Hi," she heard Brooke's voice calling out. "I was hoping we'd get to see you guys tonight." She bent down to hug Lindsay while Eleanor greeted one of the Johnsons' other friends sitting at a nearby table.

"Charlie!" Eleanor called out in her usual flamboyant way. "How delightful to see you."

She was forced to look up to say hello. A pair of dark blue eyes raked over her; her words and breath collided and blocked her throat. She couldn't breathe, let alone talk.

Logan stood right behind his mother. Sans tie, sans jacket, and in a pair of tight-fitting jeans. Jeans? She wouldn't have thought he even owned a pair. And oh, my... A black T-shirt hugged a muscled torso in all the right places. Was it her imagination, or was it suddenly very hot in the bar?

Logan moved, muscles rippled underneath his shirt, and wow... Her heart skidded to a halt. How was she supposed to sleep that night?

With difficulty, she tore her gaze away from him to greet Caitlin. The man was ridiculously attractive and had the most extraordinary effect on her insides.

Lindsay's eyes were dancing with mirth. She held out her hand to Logan with a sideways look in Charlie's direction. "Logan, hi. I've heard quite a lot about you, actually."

"I can image," sniffed his mother and sat down next to Lindsay. "Charlie, I can only apologize for my son, thinking that I'd set him up with you. Yes, he's told me. And why he would think you're a man, I have no idea."

Logan pulled out the chair next to Charlie, and again, she couldn't help but notice his stiff movements. Wincing, he sat down, his leg brushing against hers.

"There, right there," his mother said, pointing at his face, "is the reason I made an appointment for him. He's been in pain for the last six months."

For the life of her, Charlie couldn't get a word out. Heat waves radiating from Logan's body in her direction were having the strangest effect on her vocal cords.

"How did you hurt your back?' Lindsay asked him.

"I tripped while hiking," he said curtly, clearly uncomfortable talking about it.

"He has this beautiful cabin near a river; we often join him there," Eleanor said. "But he doesn't switch off nearly enough. He probably hurt himself because he was dead on his feet," his mother added. "He never stops working."

"Mom, that's enough." Logan got up, his movements stiff. "What can I get you all to drink?"

Everyone gave an order and he walked away.

"Charlie, I'm really sorry about this afternoon," Eleanor said, watching her son's retreating back. "He's in so much pain, but he's a workaholic and never takes time to go and see a therapist or a doctor; he makes me so mad."

Charlie shrugged. "We've had one session, but it's not enough to make a difference. I would've preferred to see him tomorrow and to also have a session on Sunday. And ideally, in a week's time again. I could give him names of therapists in Seattle, of course, but it's clear he doesn't think the therapy can help. Anyway, tell me about your Pilates class," she asked Eleanor. It was a favorite topic of the vivacious older woman, and thankfully she launched into a hilarious account of her last session.

They were all giggling when Logan returned to the table with their drinks on a tray. He bent slightly forward to put the tray down but wincing, he placed it way too close to the side. Charlie quickly grabbed the tray, to prevent it from tipping and sending all the drinks to the floor, then moved it to the middle of the table.

"Thank you," he said after everyone had taken their drinks.

"Charlie says you should see her tomorrow and Sunday, as well," his mother said.

He frowned. "Well, today's session was a waste of time...I'm still in pain. I can't see—"

Keeping her eyes on her drink, she interrupted, trying to explain the process. "You may not feel it yet, but your body has already begun the healing process. Two more sessions over the weekend will make all the difference. And I can give you contact details of therapists you can see in Seattle in a week's time."

"Hi, Charlie," someone called out. Tod, the owner of the bar, walked toward them. Either he or his partner, Larry, usually stopped by their table on a Friday night for a quick chat.

"Hi, Tod, lovely evening." She smiled.

"Tod," Lindsay interrupted, "this is Eleanor's son, Logan. Tell him about your back."

"Lindsay, don't…" Charlie tried to stop her sister, but Tod was always ready to tell everyone about Charlie's 'miracle hands,' and he immediately launched into an explanation of how he'd hurt his back.

"And then someone told me to try Charlie here. I have to confess"—he winked—"I was very skeptical, but I was in so much pain, I was willing to try just about anything." Before he could continue, though, someone called him away and with a mock salute, he left.

Eleanor opened her mouth, but Logan stopped her with his hand. "Mom, enough. Can we please talk about something else?"

Some of their other friends also arrived, chairs were moved, and Charlie ended up squashed in between the corner of the room and Logan's chair. She was now even closer to him than before, and couldn't get away from his leg pressed against hers. Help.

A frantic waving of a hand drew her attention to the bar. Lilly was there with some of her friends, and when she caught Charlie's eye, she pointed toward Logan, pressed her hand on her heart, and wiggled her eyebrows.

Charlie frowned at her, but Lilly kept grinning. Charlie swallowed a groan. She was never going to hear the end of this.

Charlie was driving him crazy. Under the table, his leg was happily resting against hers. She'd tried several times to move her chair, but there really wasn't any place to move to. This close, the scent of roses emanating from her was difficult to ignore.

Nearly everyone in the little bar knew Charlie. All through the evening, several people had stopped by their table, and each time, she'd get up and talk and listen. She was a toucher—she would either hug the person she was talking to or put a hand on an arm, and everyone who had been in her sphere would leave with a lighter step.

He made an effort to look around him, anything to keep himself from drooling over the softness of her skin.

Everyone was having a good time. His mom and sister were obviously happy. He was so glad for Brooke. The untimely death of her husband two years before had been such a shock to all of them. Fortunately, his mom lived literally next door and was able to help Brooke with Connor, who at the time, had only been four years old.

Next to him, Charlie laughed and his gaze returned to her as if on autopilot. Head thrown back, another pair of mini-chandeliers dangling on her ears, the bangles jingling cheerily on her slender arms, she took his breath away.

She'd changed into something even more ethereal that night. Underneath a see-through, shiny top, was another figure-fitting top, so it wasn't as if the outer layer was too revealing, but he still had trouble looking her in the eye. His gaze kept straying to where the glittering top dipped ever so slightly down to reveal the outline of a pair of beautiful breasts.

Damn it to hell, he was aching for her and she was having the time of her life, smiling and joking and seemingly oblivious to him. Well, he'd have to do something about that.

She was wearing another layered skirt, but different to the one she'd worn that morning; this one ended above her knee, leaving a pair of gorgeous legs bare.

Someone on his other side of the table asked him about his work in Seattle and ever so casually he let his other hand drop on Charlie's leg. Under his fingers, muscles tensed and because he was sitting so close to her, he caught the hitch in her throat.

One of her hands grabbed his and tried to remove it from her leg, but he caught her fingers in his and held on tightly.

"What are you doing?" she whispered.

He turned his head. "What time tomorrow?"

"What do you mean?"

"Well, you're the one who insists on seeing me again over the weekend. So, what time? Ten?"

She stopped trying to loosen her hand and nodded. "What, changed your mind?"

Her eyes really were the most extraordinary hue of blue. A man could easily drown in those depths.

Her tongue slipped out and she licked her lower lip.

"Damn, you're killing me," he groaned before he dropped her hand and grabbed his beer with both hands.

Charlie exhaled slowly. Oh, my word, she wouldn't be surprised if she'd burst into flames. She had no idea why this man had the ability to turn her insides to mush, but she was a quivering mess and the night was still young. Listening to her instincts—that was what she should be doing, but where were they when she needed them?

And where was Lindsay? She had to get out of there before she did something completely stupid, like ending up on Logan's lap.

Her sister wasn't at the table, and frantically, she searched through the throng of people in the pub. Finally, she saw Lindsay heading back toward their table, but something was wrong. Even in the dim light of the pub, she could see her sister was pale.

"I have to get to my sister," Charlie said, and tried to move her chair.

Logan looked at her. "What's wrong?"

"I have to get to Lindsay," she repeated urgently.

Logan got up quickly and moved out of her way. Lindsay was in Charlie's arms before she took another step.

"What happened?"

"He…he's found me, Charlie. He knows where I am!" she repeated over and over.

With her arms around her sister, Charlie quickly walked them out of the bar. They'd strolled over to meet there earlier—it was such a lovely evening—but now she rather wished they'd taken the car.

"I can take you home," Logan said, behind her. "My car is parked right here." He motioned toward a black sports car.

Charlie didn't even think to protest. How was it possible that Lindsay's ex-boyfriend had discovered their whereabouts? They'd been so careful. Not even their closest friends back in South Africa knew where they were going.

She helped Lindsay into the back of the car and slid in next to her. Logan nodded as if he understood her reluctance to leave her sister, even for a minute.

"It's not far—down the street and then the second one to your right," she said, holding tightly on to Lindsay, who was shaking like a leaf.

Charlie took Lindsay's hand. "Sweetie, what happened?"

Lindsay opened her phone. "Look at the last email," she hiccuped.

You didn't really think I'd just let you go? I'm coming for you.

As Charlie read the words, fury at this man, who'd nearly destroyed her sister two years ago with his verbal abuse, threatened to choke her. She had to take a deep breath. "It's an email, not a message. At least he doesn't have your phone number. We'll get you another email address immediately. He's not getting close to you ever again, I promise you."

Lindsay continued to shiver. Charlie wanted to scream out her frustration. How did this happen?

Logan didn't talk until they stopped in front of the small cottage she'd inherited from their mother's sister, Aunt Charlene.

Before she could touch the door, Logan was opening it. She thought he'd leave as soon as he'd dropped them, but he held out his hand. "Key? I'll open the front door."

She handed him her bag while helping Lindsay out of

the car.

"How did he find us, Charlie?" Lindsay sniffled. "How? Nobody back in South Africa knows where we are. Just Gavin."

Logan had opened the front door and was waiting for them, her bag still in his hands.

Charlie hugged Lindsay tightly as they walked into the house. "I don't know, but you're going to get into bed and you're not to worry about this, okay? I'll phone Gavin…"

"Please phone him now?" Lindsay pleaded, and sat down on the couch.

Logan still had her bag and he silently handed it to her. "Thanks, Logan, we'll be okay now," she said, while taking out her phone, and she dialed Gavin's number.

"I have nowhere I need to be right now. Let me help. I'll make tea," he said. "Kitchen?"

Before she could refuse, Gavin answered on the other side of the line. She sat down next to Lindsay on the couch. "Gavin—"

"What happened?" he interrupted.

"It's Mark. He's contacted Lindsay."

"How?"

"By email."

Gavin swore out loud. "What the hell?"

"I have no idea how…"

Gavin inhaled sharply. "My email account was hacked a few days ago. The possibility that Mark Taylor could be involved didn't even cross my mind. It's been two years! But damn it, it must have been his doing. He's got enough money to pay someone to do something like this; he's too damn stupid to do it himself. I can't believe he'll go to such lengths, though. But that was the only way he could've found out what her new email address is."

"It makes sense," Charlie said. "We don't send emails to friends back in South Africa because we've been worried about hacking—we message or phone. Neither of us even have a website at the moment, even though we know how important it is nowadays."

"How's Lindsay?" Gavin wanted to know.

"You can imagine."

"I'll book a flight… How the hell do I even get to you guys?

"It's a twenty-six-hour flight," Charlie replied. "Cape Town to Newark and then you fly to Bozeman. From there you take the I-90 west. It's about half an hour's drive to Livingston and then another twenty minutes to Alisson."

"Okay, let me see what I can do. I'll let you know when I'll be arriving. I've been thinking about visiting anyway."

There was so much she wanted to ask her brother, but she didn't want to upset Lindsay any further. "Okay, let me know—we can come and pick you up."

"Don't bother, I'll just get a car."

They talked for a few more minutes before they ended the call.

"What did he say?" Lindsay asked, still shivering.

"His email account was hacked," Charlie said as Logan came back with a tray in his hands. "Gavin now thinks it was probably Mark."

"So, he can find me?" Lindsay whispered, her hands gripping her upper arms.

Charlie grabbed her sister's hands. "Mark Taylor will have to go through me to get to you, and trust me, I've been ready for him for the last two years. Now I want you to take a deep breath…" She waited for Lindsay to inhale. "And exhale. Look at me." She took her sister's face in her hands. "You are beautiful and strong and independent." It was a refrain she'd been telling Lindsay over and over again over the last two years.

"You have your own successful shop and you've managed to do that all on your own. He doesn't have power over you anymore, remember? Focus on your breathing—that is the only important thing right now."

She kept her hands on either side of Lindsay's face and

breathed in and out with her until she could finally see Lindsay's shoulders relaxing. "There we go," she crooned. "You can do this; you've been doing this for the last two years, remember?"

"Have some tea," Logan said. "My mom swears by the magic of a cup of tea."

"And so do we." Charlie smiled. She wasn't sure why he was still around, but at the moment, another presence in the house was really comforting.

Logan handed Lindsay a cup. "You okay?"

Lindsay nodded. "I will be." With her cup in her hand, she got up and looked at Logan. "Thanks for bringing us home, I really appreciate it. I'm going to bed, Charlie."

"I'll be up shortly," she replied.

Lindsay nodded and left the room.

"Drink your tea," Logan said, pushing a cup into her hands. "You're shaking."

"I'm just so mad," she muttered, taking a sip. "This isn't 'just' tea, is it?" she gasped.

"You both needed something a little stronger." He sat down on the couch beside her. "Is there something I can do?"

She shook her head. "Lindsay and I moved here from South Africa two years ago. Lindsay's last boyfriend was verbally abusive and… I won't bore you with the details. Fortunately, at the time, I'd just inherited this house and the building where I have my practice and Lindsay her shop from our aunt Charlene, my mom's sister. I was still considering my options when Lindsay arrived on my doorstep out of the blue after I hadn't seen her for more than a year."

She closed her eyes and shook her head. The sight of her deathly pale sister on her porch, holding on to her bag for dear life, wasn't a sight she would ever forget.

"Anyway, it was an easy decision to move here. Our mom was American and we were actually born here before our parents moved to South Africa, so we have US passports. It made the whole thing much easier."

"Your parents—are they still in South Africa?"

"No, they…there was a terrible car accident a few years before—we lost them then. So besides Gavin, there was no one keeping us in South Africa."

"Is this the first time this Mark has contacted her since you moved here?"

She nodded. "Yes. Although, I honestly didn't think he'd still be looking for her; we closed all our social media accounts when we moved. I've since opened one for my services and Lindsay has one for her shop, but we still don't have personal ones. It's been a difficult road for her since then—he just about destroyed her self-esteem—but she's been so brave, so damn determined to get her life back, and just when she was finally relaxing, the bastard contacts her."

"So how did he get hold of her details now? You mentioned hacked emails?"

"Yes, Gavin thinks he hacked his emails." She put down her cup and stood up. "Wow, sorry, I didn't mean to go on and on like that. You should go back to the bar. Thanks for bringing us home."

"Of course. I'm so sorry about your sister. What about you? Are you okay?"

She quickly moved to the front door and opened it. "I will be. Once Gavin gets here, everything will be fine. Look, you don't have to keep to our appointment tomorrow if you'd rather not—"

"I'll see you at tomorrow at ten," he interrupted. "Please let me know if there is anything I can do."

"Thank you. I appreciate it."

He took a step forward, but as she was closing the door, he turned around and slipped a hand underneath her hair, cupping her face. "I hate seeing you distressed…" he whispered before his lips touched hers briefly. Warm, urgent lips met hers for about a millisecond but when he lifted his head, she had to grab the door so that she didn't fling herself in his arms.

"Good night," she managed.

"Sweet dreams." He smiled before he turned around and walked toward his car.

Her knees buckling, Charlie gripped the door as she watched him leave. Sweet dreams? There'd be nothing sweet about any of her dreams.

CHAPTER 4

Saturday morning Logan was up early and he went for a walk. His back was still a problem and he didn't feel ready to go for his usual run. It was another beautiful summer's day. He breathed in the fresh, early morning air, his gaze on beautiful mountains surrounding the town. He loved growing up here.

Although his dad had been a property developer, he also had a ranch nearby. And Logan lived for the weekends when he and his dad would go to the ranch. He loved the open spaces, the horses, the beautiful, old ranch house. All of that had changed when his dad died, though.

His mom had sold the ranch and their lives changed forever. Way back then, he was furious about her decision, but he later understood it hadn't been possible for her to keep a ranch going while supporting two children and pursuing her own career.

Lately, he been thinking about the ranch. He'd also discovered the same ranch was on the market at the moment. This bit of information shouldn't interest him, but it did. And it was ridiculous. His life was in Seattle. Owning a ranch near Alisson made no sense.

As he neared his mother's house, he turned his body

31

from side to side. It was probably his imagination, but his back felt slightly better. Slightly.

It was only after he'd left Charlie's house last night on his way to pick up his mom and sister that he'd acknowledged to himself the only reason he'd joined his mother and sister last night was because he'd hoped to see Charlie again.

Thoughts and dreams of her had kept him up most of the night, and left him restless and out of sorts.

What the hell was wrong with him? Apart from the fact that she was so not the type of woman he normally dated, she lived here and he was in Seattle.

He still remembered the way she burst out laughing when he'd suggested she was in on his mother's scheme to get them together. Getting married wasn't something she was interested in, she'd said. So what did that mean?

That question had been bothering him since the day before. She didn't want to get married, or she didn't date? And why was he thinking about it? Thinking about her?

And who the hell was Gavin?

When he opened the kitchen door, his mother was making coffee.

"Morning, Mom, you're up early," he said, kissing her on her cheek.

She leaned against him for a moment. "I'm so happy you're here." Her eyes searched his face. "Have you heard anything from Charlie this morning?"

He'd dodged his mom and Lindsay's questions the night before; he didn't feel comfortable discussing what Charlie had told him. It's possible his mother knew about her past, but he'd rather not say anything. "I'm sure they will tell you in time. You'll be glad to know I have another appointment with Charlie this morning," he added, changing the topic.

"Promise me you'll keep an open mind, please?" his mom implored. "It's a very different technique to what you're probably used to, but it works. I couldn't move my head properly from side to side without pain, but now, for the first time in years, I can go to sleep without having to take a pill."

"I'm going, Mom, although I still don't see how it can help me. A good massage makes sense. But how the feather-like movements she performs on my back can cure me, I have no idea."

"Just you wait. But she's lovely, isn't she? And no, I'm not playing matchmaker; you are way too staid for her."

He frowned. "She's gorgeous, yes, I've noticed. But I don't know why you'd call me staid," he grumbled, and sat down at the table. Something smelled wonderful.

She smiled. "I've got muffins—want one? Don't worry," she added with a sigh when she noticed his wary glance, "I didn't make them. There is a lovely little shop not far from here where I buy most of my meals."

He grinned. His mom could do many things; cooking wasn't one of them. "Then yes, please, I'm hungry." On any normal day, he usually only had coffee in the morning, but ever since he'd arrived back home, "normal" wasn't a word he could use to describe anything, least of all his feelings.

The front door opened. "Mom?" his sister called, and seconds later she and Connor appeared at the kitchen door.

As soon as the little boy saw him, he rushed forward. "Uncle Logan! You have to come and see my treehouse. Mommy made one for me!"

While talking non-stop, the little boy moved close to him. "Will you, Uncle Logan?"

Logan put his arm around Connor. "Of course, I will. Mmmh, Mommy made the tree house?"

"Yes!" The little boy laughed. "It doesn't look like a tree-house tree house, you know? But it's my tree house."

He caught his sister's eye. "So how did Mommy make the tree house?"

"She used a hammer. And very bad words," the little

boy whispered loudly. "But I'm not supposed to tell."

They all laughed and Logan caught his sister's hand. "I'm here till tomorrow. Tell me if there is anything I can help you with? I've never built a tree house, but I could try."

"Connor seems to be happy with my efforts." Brooke patted his arm. "Besides, it would seem you're helping quite a few people over this weekend. I sent Charlie a message this morning, asking what happened last night."

"So you have news? I've just been asking Logan about it…" his mother said before she turned to her grandson.

"Connor, why don't you go and play with Granny's Lego inside?" his mom asked the little boy.

With a dramatic sigh, Connor turned away. "That means I'm not supposed to hear what the grown-ups are saying," he told Logan as he left the room.

"You know way too much for a five-year-old." Brooke laughed.

As soon as Connor had left, his mom asked again. "What happened? Don't tell me it's her ex-boyfriend…?"

Brooke pulled out a chair and sat down. "Unfortunately, it is. He's contacted her, threatening her; Charlie said she was so upset. Thank you, again, Logan, for taking them home and that you stayed for a bit. I heard you even made tea."

"The poor child," his mother muttered. "Lindsay has never told us the whole story—just said she wasn't safe with her last boyfriend. She's been looking well lately, but when they arrived here two years ago, she was so pale, had dark circles under her eyes. She kept looking over her shoulder. Shame, she was a shadow of the woman she is today. I can't believe he's been looking for her all this time."

Logan checked his watch and got up. "My appointment with Charlie is at ten." He also wanted to speak to one of his friends from school who was the county sheriff. He'd feel better if he knew someone else was keeping an eye on the two sisters.

"Mmm, Charlie again?" Brooke grinned. "Mom, wasn't it yesterday he was still adamant she can't help him?"

"I may have overreacted…" he began but both women burst out laughing. Seriously?

As he left the kitchen, he could hear their giggling all the way up the stairs. He had a quick shower before he got dressed. As he left the room, his eye caught his overnight bag. Hadn't he planned to leave today? Yet here he was, willingly returning to see Charlie.

Charlie arrived at the practice with half an hour to spare before Logan's appointment. Lilly didn't work over weekends, so she had the place to herself for a while. She needed a few quiet moments to try and restore her equilibrium.

Because of a lack of sleep, she was irritated, grumpy, and upset. Mostly because she so worried about Lindsay's ex who'd contacted her again, but she also didn't know what to do about the strange feelings inside her caused by the mere thought of Logan Johnson.

She hadn't wanted to leave Lindsay alone at home, but fortunately Brooke had phoned to say she'd pop in to see her sister.

So at least she didn't have to worry about Lindsay; she only had to face Logan Johnson again after last night's kiss. Okay, so it wasn't really a kiss, but their lips had met and…

She opened the window and inhaled the fresh air. She and Lindsay hadn't initially known how they would feel about living in a small, rural town. Back in South Africa, they had lived in Johannesburg, a big bustling city, so they thought they might eventually decide to move to Bozeman or maybe even Seattle in the nearby state of Washington.

But both of them quickly came to love life in the small town. Brooke and Eleanor were their first clients, and through them they'd been introduced to the whole community. And now she couldn't imagine living anywhere else.

Initially they'd struggled to get clients, but over time they'd gained the trust of the town's people and lately they were also getting queries from people from the nearby town of Livingston, and even from Bozeman.

She pressed her hand to her stomach. These crazy feelings Logan had stirred deep within her were definitely a first. It wasn't as if she hadn't been attracted to a man before, but what happened to her when Logan Johnson was around could by no means merely be described as simple attraction.

For goodness' sake, if she wasn't mistaken, she had butterflies on her stomach. Ridiculous. Who still got butterflies in their tummy at nearly thirty?

There was a soft knock on her door and she turned around quickly. And there he was. Dressed in a cobalt blue shirt and jeans, he simply took her breath away.

"You're early," she got out.

With his eyes on her, he entered the room. "Good morning, Charlene."

She had to swallow a few times before she could talk. "You can call me Charlie."

He nodded. "Charlie."

His voice sent shivers down her spine. Oh, get a grip. He was just another client. She motioned toward the table. "Please lie down on your stomach; I'll be with you shortly."

She waited for him to move away from the door before she briskly left the room. There was no good reason to leave now, except that she had to try and breathe.

Inhale, exhale. He was simply another client in pain. One who needed her professional help, not her drooling over him.

Logan was lying on his stomach, his eyes closed, when he heard the jingle of her bangles and her soft tread next to the table. Strangely enough, he was quite relaxed today.

She didn't talk but he felt her nearness, smelled the subtle scent of roses she seemed to carry around her. For a few moments, he sensed her hands above his body before she touched him.

His eyes were still closed, but he could still clearly see her in his mind's eye. Today she was wearing a soft blue, glittery top with yet another long, gauzy, blueish, layered skirt. The top had tiny buttons from top to bottom and his fingers twitched the minute he'd noticed this. On her ears were a pair of huge, golden hoops. No mini-chandeliers today.

Exquisite. Beautiful. Sexy as hell.

He exhaled slowly. Whether he liked it or not, he'd been waiting for this moment since he'd left the day before—to be close to her, to feel her hands on him, to inhale her uniqueness.

"Okay, now try and relax. I'm leaving the room again to allow time for your body to integrate the effects of the set of rolling movements I've just preformed. The basic idea is to prompt your muscles and tissue in the body to repair and heal." Her voice was husky and she hastened away.

Again, she'd barely touched him, but the blood was pounding through his veins, making such a noise, he couldn't hear anything else. He was aching to touch her, to kiss her, to make love to her...

He swore loudly and turned his head. Damn it to hell! What was it with this woman? Yes, she was gorgeous, but it wasn't as if he hadn't met beautiful woman before. But thoughts of her had taken over his brain. He never stopped working and was always either checking emails or sending emails while constantly keeping his eye on the markets. But since yesterday, he couldn't be bothered even to open his laptop. That had never happened before.

"You still okay?" She was back.

He grunted, unable to respond. It had been a mistake to return this morning; he should've stuck to his decision to go back to Seattle. Do not get entangled with a woman who even remotely resembled his mother or sister—that had been his motto ever since he could remember.

He loved them dearly, but they drove him nuts. Neither one of them ever did anything close to normal and both seemed to thrive on chaos.

Order—that was what he craved in life. Not chaos. And if that made him boring, as his sister had declared, so be it. He preferred the word "steady." In the very unpredictable financial world he worked in, clients depended on his steadiness.

Even his style was minimalist. Whether it was his clothing or the décor of his home or office, he preferred clean lines and the bare necessities. After years of living with his mother's flamboyant array of colorful cushions and throws, he'd made sure there were none in his own house.

And if he'd needed another reason to stay away from Charlie, he just had to remember her house. He swore there were cushions of every color of the rainbow in the living room.

"Okay, I'm leaving again. Just relax." And with a swoosh of her skirt, she was gone.

Cursing, he banged his head on the bed. *Get a grip, Johnson, damn it!*

CHAPTER 5

With her hand on the knob, Charlie pressed her forehead against the door. Another quick session and she could send the man on his way. She could do this.

She'd been talking to herself all morning in a desperate attempt to keep her emotions in check. Each time she worked on his body, her hands barely touched him, but every single time, she was worried she'd burst into flames.

Where was the little voice she needed to stop her from doing stupid things? Because it would seem since Logan had arrived on her doorstep, her instincts had gone completely haywire.

Maybe it was because she hadn't been on a date for... When was the last time she'd been on a date? Kissed someone? Had sex? Six months ago? She couldn't even remember. Maybe that was the problem. There weren't that many prospects in a small town like Alisson, but then maybe she was too picky and not really interested. She wasn't looking for a husband, but maybe she should think about dating again. At least then she wouldn't melt at the mere sight of the next attractive man.

She opened the door. Logan was still lying on his stomach, his eyes closed. He was snoring softly. Stunned, she stared at him. Here she was, all jittery and flustered and he was snoring away.

Quickly, she moved closer. The sooner this session ended, the better for the poor butterflies on her stomach—at this point they had to be exhausted.

She put her hands on his back, trying not to look at his firm butt; however, like all the other times that day, her eyes kept straying in that direction. It wasn't difficult to imagine touching…

"Are we done yet?" he asked groggily, and she just about jumped out of her skin.

He turned his head; blue eyes met hers. "Why so skittish?" His voice was husky and sexy, sending those stupid butterflies into a frenzy again.

"Nearly," she got out, and with her eyes still on his, she dropped her hands on his back. Only, they didn't end up there but on his very firm buttocks. Inhaling, she quickly lifted her hands. "I'm…sorry," she muttered while moving her hands to where his injury was.

It had just been a moment but oh, my word… Firm, muscled, exactly what she'd imagined. Her breasts felt heavy. Her nipples hardened.

Damn it, if she didn't stop touching him now, she might just end up doing something completely inappropriate.

She glanced at him again, only to find his eyes still on hers. Was it her imagination or had they darkened?

Praying for her body not to respond further, she performed a quick succession of rolling movements before she dropped her hands. "There you go." Oh my word, again the husky voice. Seriously?

She turned away. "Thanks again for helping us last night—we really appreciate it."

"So you've said." He was already up and right behind her.

When she turned around, they were standing toe to toe. "I'm…" Mesmerized, she stared at his mouth. Last night's kiss wasn't really a kiss, just a nibble, really. But if she were honest, and this close to him she had no other option but to be honest, she'd like another taste. The thought of kissing him again had kept her awake most of the night, anyway.

He lifted his hand and cupped her face; the room fell silent. *Say something.* She couldn't kiss him again. It would be a disaster. "Logan..." was all she managed.

His eyes dropped and the one corner of his mouth lifted.

She looked down to see what had caught his attention. And damn...her nipples were clearly straining against her top. *Help!* She'd never, ever had this problem. Blushing furiously, she tried to move away, but he lifted his other hand, as well, to touch her cheek.

"Damn, Charlie, you're driving me crazy." He bent his head. "I have to..." His lips were barely touching hers, waiting, asking permission.

Nodding, she licked her dry lips and with a groan, he pulled her head closer and kissed her.

By the time his lips closed over hers, he was desperate. The madness that had filled his every waking moment since he'd met her was egging him on and he simply had no choice.

He swallowed her gasp, his tongue quickly finding its way into the warm, wet depths of her mouth. The scent of roses seeped through his skin, joined the blood rushing through his veins, and within seconds he was in danger of losing control.

Satin and silk, creamy lines and toned angles, she was all woman. Her mouth was supple and warm and he was lost. Angling his head, he deepened the kiss and pulled her closer. Soft breasts fitted perfectly against his body.

His heart was beating so loudly no other sound penetrated the sensory bubble they were in. All that actually registered were the delicate smoothness of her skin, the sexy sound of her breath, the intoxicating taste of her lips.

Somewhere, warning signals flashed, trying to get his attention, but he ignored it. His only objective was to try and assuage the gnawing ache deep inside him, and she was the only one who could do that.

After long minutes, he eventually lifted his head, breathing heavily. Her mouth was wet and swollen with his kisses, her eyes liquid ink, desire still lurking in the depths.

"Damn, you're killing me," he groaned. His gaze dropped to where her beautiful breasts strained against the top, the hard beads tantalizingly visible.

"I have to…" He cupped his hand around her breast. It was an exact fit.

She whimpered, the most beautiful sound he'd ever heard. With a groan, he kissed her again. But now that he'd had a taste of her, he wanted more. Desperately, his lips glided over her chin, exploring every curve and velvety line of her throat as he discovered new textures and scents. And still he wanted more.

"Logan…" Her fingers were in his hair, spurring him on. He moved her top aside, his lips finding the enticing curve of her breast. Joyously he nibbled his way over her satiny softness down to those hard, little nubs waiting for his attention.

When his mouth finally closed over her breast, the sound of a groan filled the air around them. He wasn't sure whether it was his or hers, but hungrily, he moved the last barrier aside so that he could taste her flesh.

This was what he'd dreamed about the whole of last night. He suckled and licked and feasted on her breasts until she shuddered beneath his mouth. But although the ache inside him had been appeased somewhat, he wanted more. Much, much more. His hand trailed down her skirt.

The only voice she could hear was the one spurring her on to drag Logan to the ground and have her way with him. But finally, sanity prevailed when a lonely, rational little voice managed to penetrate the lustful fog she'd been in since Logan's lips had found hers. She started pulling away.

Her fingers were still curled up in his hair but somehow, she had to put a stop to this. "Logan…" Her voice sounded raspy.

"What?" he growled, his mouth still around her breast.

"This is madness, we…you…"

Finally, he lifted his head. Untamed passion shone from the blue depths of his eyes for a moment, before he stepped back.

Gulping in air, she tried to fasten the buttons of her blouse, but her hands were so unsteady, the simple task was beyond her.

Cursing, he moved closer again and brushed her hands aside. "Let me."

Logan's fingers were shaking so much, he also struggled with the simple task of putting a button in a hole. As if that wasn't bad enough, his fingers kept touching the silky curve of her breast in the process. Passion lurked just below the surface and he knew if he didn't get out of there fast, he wouldn't be closing buttons, but opening them.

Both of them were still breathing heavily. When he was done, he touched her face. "You're right, this is madness. You're beautiful and you make me ache in places I didn't know was possible. But you're so not the type of woman I normally date…"

Her eyes narrowed and she stepped back without saying a word.

He put his hands in the pockets of his jeans. "I like my life uncomplicated and tidy. And neat. And without scatter cushions in every damn color of the rainbow." He frowned. "Look at you—who wears glitter during the day? It's weird."

Before he could complete his sentence, she'd marched to the door and was opening it. "Goodbye, Logan. I hope your back feels better soon."

He felt like a jerk. Damn it, he was a jerk. "I'm sorry. I'm just trying to be honest here. I'm not interested in anything permanent…"

"Neither am I, you egotistical idiot. Now get out."

It was only when he looked at her again, as he walked past her, that he saw the glimmer of tears in her eyes. He stopped but she shoved him outside and closed the door behind him.

"And then he had the gall to ask me who wears glitter during the day!" Charlie was still so mad, she was pacing up and down their small living room.

"So, just to be clear, we don't like him anymore?" Lindsay asked, obviously highly amused. "He was very kind last night."

"I know, but then this morning…" She threw up her hands.

Lindsay cleared her throat. "What I'm still not sure about is what happened before he told you you're not his type?"

Charlie stopped her pacing for a moment. It was nearly six and she'd just arrived back home. A few more clients had needed her that morning, but afterward, she had still been so worked up, she'd ended up cleaning her office.

She hadn't planned on telling Lindsay what had happened. Saying it out loud would make it more…more real. But of course, Lindsay knew something was wrong the minute she'd stepped into the house just now.

But it was real, damn it—he'd kissed her, not the other way around. He'd touched her and she'd let him because she'd never been so moved by a kiss before.

"I mean, if, say for instance, he kissed you, I could understand…" Lindsay said.

Charlie looked up quickly. "How did you know?"

Giggling even harder now, Lindsay jumped up. "So that's why you're so upset. The man kissed you and you liked it."

Charlie flopped down on a chair. "Okay, he kissed me. Only to tell me afterward I was not his type."

"Did he stop the kiss or did you?"

"I stopped it! It was a moment of madness and he agreed."

"So why are you so upset?"

"I'm not upset, I'm mad," Charlie grumbled. She tossed her hair back. "I've already forgotten about the whole thing and I hope never to hear the name Logan Johnson again. How was lunch? How are you?" She'd checked in on Lindsay throughout the day and was so happy to hear that Brooke had also invited her for a meal.

"It was lovely, thanks. Brooke is such a sweet person and I adore her little boy. I'm okay, for the moment. I have a new email address and I've already sent it to everyone who uses it. Fortunately, most of our clients use the general email I use for work."

"Just promise me you won't go anywhere on your own, please? Not until we're sure what that man is up to."

Lindsay shook her head. "I still can't believe he's been looking for me all this time."

"You don't need a degree in psychology to know he is a textbook narcissist and psychopath. He has to get in the last word. But nothing is going to happen to you as long as I'm here, okay?"

Lindsay nodded. "I've been thinking… You remember the self-defense classes I took after we arrived here?"

"I do. You were very good at it, I remember."

"Well, I've phoned them again. Unfortunately, Phil, the guy who helped me before, has apparently left for the big city, but someone else has now taken over his dojo. The new guy teaches self-defense as well as some other martial arts like karate. There is a self-defense class Monday afternoons after work. I was thinking of joining and was hoping I could persuade you to come with me?"

"Of course, I will. It'll be good exercise, as well."

"Thanks again for being so sweet last night. It's been two years since I've last heard anything from him. I just didn't expect to see an email from him, you know?" Lindsay sighed. "I'm mostly upset because just one line from him freaked me out. I thought I was better. I've seen a psychologist, I've taken self-defense classes, I do meditation for goodness' sake; I shouldn't have been so upset. But in that second while I was reading his words, fear grabbed me at the throat and I simply forgot everything I've learned over the past two years."

Charlie got up and put her arms around her sister. "You are brave and beautiful and intelligent—you've got this."

With a sniff, Lindsay returned her hug before she stepped back. "Thanks, sis. I am so grateful I have you in my life. I've been thinking about our Seattle trip. Now that Gavin will be visiting, I should probably stay here. Will you be okay going on your own?"

"Let's see when Gavin arrives. I can always join the meeting via Zoom or Skype; I don't have to go."

"You've been talking about meeting other Bowen therapists since we've arrived here. I don't think you should cancel."

Charlie frowned. "But with Mark…"

Lindsay squared her shoulders. "I've decided I'm not giving Mark Taylor any more power to disrupt my life. Care to join me tonight? I'm going to the bar again."

And although that was really the very last place she wanted to be, Charlie nodded. "That's the spirit. Of course, I will."

"And what if He We Won't Name is there?"

"He's probably back in Seattle already. So come on, I'm

going to wear something glittering and outrageous!"
    Lindsay giggled. "As if that will be surprising."

CHAPTER 6

Logan rolled over to his side and opened his eyes. For a moment, he was disoriented. Where was he? A giggle from downstairs penetrated his befuddled mind. Brooke's laugh. He sat up, running a hand through his hair.

He couldn't believe he'd fallen asleep. The only thought he'd had when he got back from Charlie's rooms that morning was to get the hell back to Seattle. But his mom had bought something for lunch, they'd had a glass of wine, and afterward he'd gone upstairs to pack. Only he'd ended up on his back on the bed and...he checked his watch. It was nearly seven; he'd slept most of the afternoon.

Damn it, he wanted to be back in Seattle tonight. Would there still be any flights this late? He'd have to check. There was knock on his door. "Are you decent?" his mother called.

He got up. "Yes, I am."

Before he'd finished getting the words out, she was in his room. She was dressed and all smiles. "I'm so glad you haven't left. Brooke and I are going out again; do you want to join us?"

He was going to say no, he wanted to make sure about

49

flights. Those were the words he'd expected to hear leaving his mouth. Instead, he smiled and said, "Yes, that sounds great. But I want to take a shower…"

"We'll meet you there, if that's okay? Same place as last night." She turned as if to leave, but then she looked over her shoulder. "Feeling better? You looked a bit…perturbed this morning after your visit to the lovely Charlie."

"Why? Did she say anything?" he quickly asked.

His mother frowned. "Don't tell me you had another fight with her? I don't know what it is with you and—"

"No, I didn't fight with her!" he called out in frustration. "Damn it, I kissed her."

His mother's mouth formed a perfectly round O, but there was no sound. Hell, he hadn't planned on saying anything about the kiss, least of all to his mother. He'd never hear the end of it.

But she shrugged. "Well, obviously you didn't like kissing her—such a pity, though. She's got spunk. Now don't be too late!" And with a wave of her hand, she left.

Didn't like kissing her? Of course, he liked kissing her, damn it—that was the whole freaking problem. He loved kissing her. *Loved*. What the hell was wrong with him? She was so not the kind of woman he should be even be thinking about, let alone be kissing.

Pulling his shirt over his head, he strode toward the bathroom. Why the hell was he still here? He closed the bathroom door behind him and leaned against it for a moment.

Because he wanted to see Charlie again. There were so many reasons to stay away from her, but he had to see her again. It was that simple.

Lindsay looked over Charlie's shoulder and waved. "You can finally relax. Eleanor and Brooke are on their way to join us and Him We Won't Name isn't with them."

Charlie smiled. The strange sensation she was experiencing couldn't be disappointment. She'd probably only drunk her first glass of wine too quickly.

The two women rushed toward them, full of smiles. "I'm so glad to see you again," Eleanor said, then hugged Lindsay. "You know we won't let anything happen to you, don't you?"

"Thanks, Eleanor. You and Brooke have been so good to us ever since we arrived here." Lindsay smiled.

"Hi, everyone," a male voice greeted them. It was Tod, the owner of the bar, and with him was another man. "I want to introduce you to another newbie in our midst, Blake Davidson. He's just moved here from New York."

It was obvious the introduction was Tod's idea. Blake smiled stiffly and nodded. "Thanks, Tod." He turned away as if to leave, but Eleanor was not put off by his unfriendly demeanor.

"Pull up a chair, why don't you? These two gals here can tell you all about our little community. They moved here two years ago from South Africa." And before Blake could open his mouth, Eleanor was up and pulling a chair closer from the table next to them.

Charlie swallowed a giggle. The poor man had no other choice but to sit down on the chair Eleanor had placed next to Charlie. He crossed his arms, clearly very uncomfortable.

"What are we drinking?" Tod asked.

Everyone placed their orders before Eleanor leaned forward. "So, what brings you to our little town?" she asked Blake.

Only Charlie probably heard the soft curse before he spoke up. "I've bought the dojo and will be teaching self-defense classes and other martial arts."

Surprised, Charlie pointed toward her sister. "Lindsay and I will be joining your self-defense class on Monday. We've just spoken about it today."

He looked at Lindsay before he answered. "It's not for

everyone, you know. But if you're sure, I'll see you Monday."

Charlie gave Blake a sideways glance. What a strange thing to say. She would think he'd be thrilled to know he had at least two new clients. Charlie tried to catch Lindsay's eye, but her sister was fidgeting with her bag.

"Hi, everyone."

Charlie looked up quickly. Logan was standing right behind Blake's chair. Her heart did a double flip before it shuddered back in place. His eyes were on her, his jaws clenched tightly together.

Charlie lifted her chin and looked away. She was not Logan's type, remember? Those were the exact words he'd used earlier. And, oh, yes—he didn't like her scatter cushions. Too bright, too many colors. She was going to listen to her instincts, damn it, and they were telling her loud and clear this man was trouble—keep away.

"Blake!" Eleanor called out gaily. "Get a chair and meet a new friend. Blake, this is my son Logan. Logan, this is Blake. He's just moved to our little town and will be teaching self-defense to Charlie and Lindsay. Isn't that lovely?"

By the time she'd finished talking, Logan had pulled up a chair and was sitting next to Lindsay.

The drinks arrived, Logan placed his order, but Charlie forced herself not to look in his direction.

Blake took a sip of the beer he'd ordered and she leaned slightly closer to him. "Eleanor can be a bit overwhelming, but she means well," she said softly.

At last the beginnings of a smile appeared on Blake's face. "I can see that. But…" He quickly looked around them and shook his head. "I'm not good with big crowds. Hashtag #introvertproblems." He smiled. "I met Tod and Larry this morning when I went for a run. They invited me for a beer, but I never expected there'd be such a crowd."

"And you certainly hadn't expected to meet new clients, it would seem."

He looked over at Lindsay. "No, it's not that that. It's just...your sister...Lindsay? Is that her name?"

"Yes, that's right. What about her?"

Blake couldn't seem to take his eyes off her sister. "She's very...delicate, isn't she?"

"Actually, she's one of the strongest people I know." She looked up to find Logan looking grimly at her. Nothing new there. She quickly turned back to Blake. "So, tell me, how did you get into this line of work?"

What the hell was so funny that she had to smile all the damn time? Logan gulped down the rest of his beer, never taking his eyes off Charlie. Tonight, she simply took his breath away.

The shimmering top she was wearing had a wide neckline, leaving her shoulders bare. He noticed the creamy satin of her skin and the ache he'd thought he'd tempered that morning was back. He'd tasted her, he'd touched her, and he couldn't think about anything else than to get his hands on her again as soon as humanly possible.

A tight band across his chest made breathing difficult. He sipped at his beer, watching her. She threw her head back and laughed at something what's-his-name next to her said. Inside of him there was a shift. What's-his-name was grinning, as well, clearly also enthralled with Charlie.

It was when she bent her head and moved closer to the guy that he'd had enough. He stood up quickly, bumping against the table in the process.

"Everything okay, Logan?" his mother asked.

"Everything is fine, Mom, I just need...I need to ask Charlie something. About...about my back."

And finally, Charlie looked at him, her eyebrows raised. "What about your back?"

"Can we talk outside?" he asked.

"I'm having a drink," she said.

"And I need your help," he insisted.

Charlie's first reaction was to throw the contents of her wine glass in Logan's face, but she was very much aware of his mom and sister watching them. Muttering an excuse, she got up quickly and stomped out of the pub. The freaking man was driving her crazy. And the fact that he looked sexy as hell in a plain, white T-shirt and a pair of tight-fitting jeans wasn't helping.

He was right on her heels and when she turned around outside, they were nearly touching.

"What…what about your back?" she got out. Again, the husky voice. Seriously?

He grabbed her hand and moved them to the side of the building. "I don't want to talk about my back. In fact, I don't want to talk at all." His hand glided up her arm and landed on her bare shoulder.

"Damn you, Logan Johnson. I'm not your type, remember? What are you still doing here, anyway? I thought you'd be back in Seattle, dining and wine-ing a neat and tidy woman who only wears black and gray."

His head bent. Warm lips grazed her shoulder. Her knees nearly buckled and she had to lean against the wall behind her.

"I know what I said, damn it," he growled, his lips trailing over her skin, "but I didn't like the way you smiled at what's-his-name in there. I haven't been able to think about anything else but kissing you, tasting you again. Did you know you smell like roses?"

And with a groan, he pulled her closer. "I want to kiss you," he whispered, waiting for her consent.

Walk away, be outraged, Logic tried to tell her. But Heart, her heart, easily won this round. Here, so close to him, all she wanted was his mouth on hers. She'd barely nodded when warm, urgent lips plundered hers mercilessly until she had to grab hold of his shoulders just to keep standing.

His skin was hot under her fingers. His muscles flexed as he moved to bring her even closer to him. And oh my. His desire throbbed intimately against her body and this time her knees did buckle.

"I want you, Charlie," he growled against her lips, moving one leg between hers. "Now."

"Even if I'm not your type?" she scolded while trying to disentangle herself from him.

"Do you think I don't know that? But damn it, I have to kiss you." Again he waited until she nodded before he cupped her face and kissed her.

Tears gathered behind her closed eyes and one or two escaped and ran down her face. He lifted his head, frowning. "You're crying."

Sniffing, she finally pushed him away. "You will have to make up your mind, Logan. You can't tell me I'm not your type, but you keep kissing me. This is me. Weird. I think that was the word you used. And yes, I wear glitter any damn time I want and I love my colored cushions. I'm not changing. For anyone. I hope your back will heal soon." And gathering her last shred of dignity, she walked away.

She blinked furiously, trying not to cry. The last thing she wanted to do was upset Lindsay any further. In any case, there was nothing to be upset about. Logan apparently liked kissing her, but he didn't like her. There wasn't anything left to say about it.

Breathing hard, Logan stared at Charlie's back until she disappeared from his sight. Then, shoving his hands into his pockets, he walked back to his car.

He'd discovered the first flight back to Seattle would be leaving early in the morning, which meant he had to stay here another night, knowing Charlie was close by. Fortunately, he'd have to leave at the crack of dawn to catch the six o'clock flight. He had to get as far away from this woman as possible. At least until his sanity returned.

He got into his car and closed the door. For a while, he sat there. What was it about her? Yes, she was beautiful, but so were many other women he knew. But there was something about her that had touched something so deep inside himself, he hadn't even known it existed.

That he could want someone like this, could crave someone's presence like this, was so surprising, it had never happened before. Muttering a string of curses, he started his car and drove away quickly. But not before he glanced back one more time. She wasn't anywhere to be seen, though. She was inside. With what's-his-name.

And he shouldn't forget about Gavin somebody, who would also be arriving later this week. His hands clutched the steering wheel tighter. Charlie with another man? The mere thought was enough to drive him crazy, damn it to hell.

He slowly drove back to his mother's house. Hopefully this madness would vanish once he was back in Seattle.

The minimalist neat and tidy monochrome décor of his house would calm his overstimulated senses as it always did. He would take a nice, normal, pretty woman out to dinner and soon he wouldn't even remember what Charlie looked like or why he'd been in such a state over her.

Yeah, right.

CHAPTER 7

Charlie smiled brightly as she walked back into the bar. Her heart was breaking, but she was not going to let Logan Johnson spoil her evening with her sister and friends. The absolute gall of the man—she wasn't his type but he wanted her? Seriously?

He made her so mad and that was what she was going to cling to. As long as she stayed angry, she could—maybe—forget how perfectly and precisely she fitted against his body; she could try not to think about his hungry kisses, the desperate urgency in his touch and the desire she'd tasted on his lips.

Oh, hell—this wasn't helping.

Eleanor was looking at her phone, frowning. As Charlie sat down, she looked up. "A message from Logan. He says he's going back home?"

Charlie shrugged and looked around her. "I don't know. What happened to Blake?"

Lindsay lifted her glass. "Not sure. He was here the one moment and then he left. Here's to us girls."

They all lifted their glasses and within minutes Eleanor had them giggling again. Charlie did her best to join in the conversation and fun but a huge hole had opened up inside of her, leaving her feeling empty and drained.

Taking a sip of her wine, she tried to shake off the silliness. This was why she didn't date, remember? She had a charmed life—she had a job she loved, wore clothes that made her happy and she shared a lovely home, colorful cushions included, with her favorite person, Lindsay. Damn it, she'd known Logan was trouble the minute he'd walked into her rooms. She should've listened to her instincts.

Brooke got up. "More drinks, everyone?"

Lindsay jumped up, as well. "Of course. Let me help you."

They left and Eleanor moved closer to Charlie. "Are you okay, love? I'm sticking in my nose where it doesn't belong, I know, but I couldn't help noticing my son had difficulty taking his eyes off you."

Smiling vaguely, Charlie took another sip of her wine. "Your imagination, I think. I'm so not his type." Where were Brooke and Lindsay? She really didn't want to talk to Eleanor about her son. But her sister and Brooke were having a lively conversation with Tod and Larry at the bar; they would not be rescuing her anytime soon.

"You know," Eleanor continued, "my husband died when Logan was about ten and Brooke eight. It was unexpected and I sort of fell apart. It was only much later I realized the devastating effect his death and my subsequent struggle to handle basic things impacted Logan. He and his dad were very close. At that point, my husband had a ranch outside town and Logan loved spending weekends and holidays there. My husband was also wonderful around the house and when I was busy with a painting, he'd made sure everything else ran smoothly."

She laughed. "I'd often burn the food or forget to do the washing or cleaning and then he'd jump in to save what could be saved. But when he was gone, especially in the beginning, I just didn't have the energy to do anything. I sold the ranch. Logan was very upset although he tried not to show it. What he did was to take on the role as caretaker—not something I immediately realized. He washed the dishes, did the laundry, made sure everything was super clean. He became obsessive about keeping everything in its place. I think it was his way of trying to control the uncontrollable. And I don't know, but I think inside of him there is still a little boy who misses his dad."

Fortunately, at that moment, Brooke and Lindsay returned with their drinks and Charlie didn't have to answer.

But later that night when she was in bed, Eleanor's words kept replaying over and over in her head. Her heart ached for the little boy who'd lost his dad and who had tried in his own way to control the uncontrollable. Was that why he still had such a tight control over his emotions?

Her phoned buzzed. Who would send her messages this time of night? Her heart skipped a beat. Maybe Gavin? Did something happen? Quickly she sat up and picked up her phone. Even before she opened it, she saw the message. It was from Logan. She'd saved his number when his mother had given it to her, but she didn't know he had hers.

Flying back early tomorrow morning

Rolling her eyes, she threw the phone down. What was she supposed to reply to such a remark?

Logan sat staring at his phone. Charlie had read his message—he could see that, but that was minutes ago, damn it. Was she seriously not going to reply? Yes, he remembered every single thing he'd said, but she had to know it hadn't been easy for him to walk away.

With a curse, he threw down his phone and headed for the shower, pulling his shirt over his head. Tonight, his mom's house was way too small and cluttered for all the emotions warring inside of him.

Earlier that night, he'd ended up walking around in the familiar streets of his boyhood. But not even the well-known sights could ease the restlessness inside him.

Charlie. *Charlie*. She was all he could think about. His hands still carried her scent and it was driving him crazy. Swearing, he marched back to his bathroom. This madness had to stop.

Not waiting for the water to heat up, he stepped under the cascading stream. Ice-cold water pounded on his back, nearly knocking out his breath. He braced himself against the tiles, remembering soft skin, short breaths, glazed eyes, trembling fingers.

Cursing, he closed the tap and grabbed a towel. How the hell was he supposed to sleep if he couldn't stop thinking about her? In his room, his eyes caught the light on his phone and with two strides he reached his bed and picked it up.

She'd replied to his message.

How's your back?

His back? What the hell? Was that all she had to say?

He leaned back against the pillows, ready to send her a scathing message. His hand stopped. His back. He sat upright again, turned to his right, then his left. It was better. Much better. There was still some discomfort but not nearly as bad as it had been on Friday while he was driving to his mom's place.

At the time the pain in his back was all he could think about—he'd been very uncomfortable. But tonight, it hadn't bothered him. Why? Because, damn it, he'd been so caught up thinking about Charlie, it hadn't registered his back wasn't bothering him. Quickly, he typed a message.

Much better, thanks. Your hocus pocus worked.

And waited. Three dots appeared, hovered, and disappeared again. Again, the three dots appeared but within seconds they were gone. He kept waiting. Nothing.

Disgusted with himself, he dropped his phone and pulled on pants before he opened his laptop. If he wasn't going to sleep, he might as well work. He hadn't even opened his laptop once over the weekend—a first for him.

Aargh! Irritated with herself, Charlie switched on the light next to her bed. Rubbing her face, she checked her watch. It was nearly four o'clock and she was still tossing and turning. A thousand little men were running around, banging on drums in her head, and no matter what she'd tried, sleep evaded her.

She'd tried to focus on her breathing. That usually did the trick but tonight nothing seemed to be able to calm the craziness in her head. The minute she closed her eyes, Logan's face was right in front of her, brooding blue eyes watching her. And then she remembered the way he'd kissed her, the way he'd held her, the way he'd made her feel.

His mother's words echoed over and over in her mind and she couldn't stop thinking how hard it had to be for him to lose his dad at such a young age. She and Lindsay had been in their twenties when their parents had died, but even then, it had been a devastating event for them. How did a little boy process such a loss?

She kept trying to remind herself over and over again he'd told her she wasn't his type, but that didn't seem to help keep the memories of the brief moments they'd been together at bay.

At least she now knew his back was better. He should really try to see another therapist as soon as possible, but she'd already told him that.

Her phone lit up and she picked it up quickly. It was another message from Logan.

On my way to the airport. Sleeping much?

Seriously? Furious with him, she quickly sent a message.

Ask someone who's your type.

She'd barely sent it when her phone rang. Logan. Of

61

course. She stared at the phone. Why was he doing this to her? The phone stopped ringing and another message appeared.

You're awake, answer, damn it.

And before she'd finished reading the words, her phone rang again. Taking a deep breath, she answered. This had to stop.

"You're not being fair," she said crossly.

"Me not fair? You're the one who's driving me nuts!" His voice in her ear sent delicious shivers down her spine.

She groaned. "What do you want?"

His deep sigh sent goose bumps all over her body. "What I want, Charlie, is you."

She closed her eyes and leaned back against the pillows. "But I'm not your type. And I'm not changing for anyone."

"But I do like your mouth. And that soft spot below your ear. And your smell—it's still with me. And I like your shoulders. Do you know when I kiss you, you make this sound in your throat? It drives me crazy."

Her body was burning up. What this man could to do her with just his voice, was ridiculous. "You can't say things like that to me, Logan. You're going back to what I'm sure is your compartmentalized and probably monochrome apartment, and tomorrow you'll put on your tie and suit and go back to your tidy workplace. And I really don't have time for this. I've finally been able to make a home for Lindsay and myself. A place where she doesn't have to be afraid of anything. I don't need complications in my life. This…what happened between us, was temporary madness. You agreed with me, remember? And it's probably because I haven't had sex in a while, you're devastatingly attractive, and I…" She closed her hand over her eyes. Oh, hell, she hadn't just said that, had she?

He chuckled. "Devastatingly attractive, uh? And how long is 'a while?'"

"Good night, Logan," she said.

"Don't hang up yet, I like talking to you."

"Well, I have work tomorrow and—"

"You're the reason I'm flying back to Seattle, you know?" He sounded cross. "I didn't want to see a therapist, I don't have time to fly home, I work! But I agreed, to please my mother. And then there you were— gorgeous, with your bangles and soft skirt and blue eyes and I…" He swore softly. "You are so beautiful."

Her heart tripped. "Don't say things like that to me!" she scolded.

In her ear, his breath hitched. After a few silent seconds, he cleared his throat. "I have to know—who's Gavin? And why was what's-his-name sitting so close to you in the pub earlier tonight?"

"Why does it matter to you who I know or talk to?"

"I don't know, damn it. Do you think I like not being able to work or think about anyone or anything else but you?"

"Logan, seriously…"

"Just tell me. Please?"

Rubbing her face, she sighed. He was driving her insane. This had to end and quickly. Her poor heart could only handle so much. "I'll tell you because I want to go back to sleep. Gavin is our brother. He stayed behind in South Africa when Lindsay and I moved here. And Blake Davidson is the new martial arts instructor in town. Lindsay took self-defense classes when we moved here. And after the message she's received from her ex-boyfriend, she reached out to the dojo where she used to train, but the previous owner left earlier this year and Blake has since taken over his dojo. She and I will be taking lessons from him from Monday. That was what he and I talked about. There—happy now?"

"So you're going to see what's-his-name on a regular basis from now on? And you want to know if I'm happy? Of course, I'm not happy! I won't be happy until…until…" He inhaled, cursing softly.

"Exactly. I'm not what you want, Logan. I'm not relationship material. And you are not part of my plans. Good night." And before she could say something stupid like 'I miss you,' she disconnected the call.

Logan thought she was beautiful. It shouldn't matter but it did. Deep inside her, something that had been wound up tightly loosened ever so slightly. Grabbing one of the pillows, she hugged it against herself.

It had to end tonight. Dreaming about Logan Johnson would only lead to heartache, she knew that. If she could now only persuade her heart to listen to this piece of logic.

Her life was great, she was happy. She didn't need this complication.

CHAPTER 8

Thursday morning, Anna, Logan's PA of seven years, knocked briskly on the door before she stepped into his office. Closing the door behind her, she crossed her arms. "Logan, I need a moment of your time."

He scowled. "I don't have a moment, damn it. I'm busy, can't you see?" He knew he was rude but at this point he didn't even care. It had been a hell of a week. He couldn't sleep, he couldn't eat, and he kept smelling roses, damn it.

But instead of retreating, as he'd hoped, Anna walked right up to his big desk, put her hands on his desk, and leaned forward on her arms. "I love you like a son, you know that. But you've been impossible this week. Poor Jenny has just left in tears and I don't think I've ever seen Peter this angry. Obviously, something happened to you between last Friday and Monday morning. The question is, what? Is it still your back? I've sent thank-you-but-this-is-over flowers to Kate." She frowned. "Or was it Yvonne? I can't keep track. So, it can't be a woman, or is it? Or don't you get enough sleep? We have to talk about this, because if you continue behaving like a spoiled brat, I'm going to quit."

Logan threw down his pen and got up. "I'm fine!" he growled.

But Anna didn't budge. "No, you're not. Is it your back? I'll make an appointment…"

"My back is actually better, thanks."

Her eyes widened in surprise. "Do you want to tell me you've seen a physiotherapist or a chiropractor? I've been trying for weeks to get you to see someone."

He put his hands in his pockets. "Actually, my mother made an appointment for me."

"But that's wonderful, Logan. So, who helped you? A physio or…"

Exasperated, he raised his hands. "I don't know why I have to tell everybody every little thing about me, but no, it was with a Bowen therapist. In Alisson."

Her mouth fell open. Okay, now all he had to do was wait for her to process this bit of information. Within seconds, her frown cleared and she smiled. "Ah, I see. And she's beautiful?"

He looked out of the window. It was another lovely summer's day, beckoning one to wander outside and enjoy the sun. Why the hell was he staring out of his window and thinking about summer? He didn't have time to think about the weather. Scowling, he turned back to Anna. "Yes, she's gorgeous, but not my type." He glanced at his watch and fastened the button on his jacket. "I have a meeting. Is everyone in the conference room?"

Still smiling broadly, she nodded. "Yes, they're waiting for you. But may I so bold and suggest another trip to Alisson this weekend? It would be to everyone's advantage. And isn't the flight to Bozeman only about an hour and a half?" And with that she turned around and left his office.

He glared at Anna's retreating back, cursing.

"I heard that!" she called before disappearing from his view.

He grabbed his laptop. Anna had been with him since

he'd started this company seven years ago. Before that, she'd been his secretary at his previous job. She was the one he counted on to make his life run smoothly—she made his appointments, she sent flowers and an apology to someone when he felt a relationship had run its course. Trust her to quickly get to the bottom of why he was feeling so out of sorts this week.

There were clients who depended on his logical, rational thinking to invest their money, but this week he'd been anything but logical and rational. He stopped at Anna's desk. "Will you please send Jenny flowers—"

"And a bottle of the best Scotch for Peter?" she added.

"Yes, please. And do get flowers for yourself, as well, okay?" He smiled.

She snorted. "Don't try those baby blues on me, I know you too well. By the way, if you give me her number, I'll make another appointment for you. You know, with the Bowen therapist for this weekend?"

"I'll make my own damn appointment," he muttered as he strolled out of her office.

Her chuckle rang in his ears all the way to the boardroom. There were way too many women in his life telling him what to do.

Thursday afternoon, just after lunch, Charlie was trying to finish an email when Lindsay knocked on her door and entered. "I don't think I want to continue with the self-defense classes."

"Why not?" Charlie asked, still concentrating on the email. "You were the one who thought it would be a good idea to sharpen your skills—why stop after just one lesson?"

"Because…" Lindsay began quite vehemently and finally Charlie looked up. Fidgeting, Lindsay pressed her lips together before she spoke again. "Maybe I overreacted when I saw Mark's email."

"If you say so. But I really enjoyed Blake's class, and you have to admit, he goes out of his way to help his students. You should re-think your decision. It's the kind of thing—"

"Why he had to pick me each time for his demonstrations, I really don't know," she interrupted Charlie.

"Maybe because you were standing in the front, closest to him?"

"Where he told me to stand! Anyway, I don't think it's really necessary at this point. Besides, Gavin will be here tomorrow and we should…I don't know? Clean his room or something."

"We cleaned his room last night, remember?"

"I know but…" Lindsay began but Charlie's phone rang.

"Don't go, let me answer this. Good afternoon, Charlie Wilson speaking. How can I help you?"

But Lindsay pointed toward her watch and left with a wave.

"Is this Charlie Wilson, Bowen therapist?" a woman asked.

"That's right. Can I help you?"

"My name is Anna Davis and I want to make an appointment for my boss for tomorrow, please?"

Charlie opened up her calendar on her laptop. "Of course. What time? And your boss' name, please?"

"Any time in the afternoon?"

Charlie chewed on her lip. She'd hoped to take tomorrow afternoon off because Gavin would be here. "It's not possible in the morning?" she tried.

"I was hoping you have an opening around four o'clock?" Anna insisted. "If that is at all possible?"

Charlie swallowed her groan. "Of course."

"That sounds perfect, thank you. I'll send you the details!" And before Charlie could respond, Anna had ended the call.

Charlie typed in "Anna's boss" on her calendar before she got up. But now she wanted to find out why Lindsay didn't want to go back to the self-defense classes.

It was late Thursday afternoon when Logan got back to his office. He was tired and irritated. Meetings were the one aspect of his work he could really do without. Why was there always an idiot hell-bent on sharing his ideas, whether it was on the topic under discussion or not?

Anna and most of the others had already left. He loosened his tie and sat down, pulling his computer closer. He wanted to get home so he could go for a run. Even if it was only a short one, it should help improve his mood. But first, he wanted to check his calendar and see what his day would look like tomorrow.

This morning he'd woken up with just one thought, and that was Charlie. He wanted to see her, touch her. He'd been contemplating returning to Alisson again. A crazy, stupid idea, he knew. He couldn't leave now; he probably had back-to-back appointments and meetings tomorrow. Besides, hadn't she told him in no uncertain terms he wasn't part of her plans?

Since he'd contacted Charlie late Saturday night, he'd forced himself not to send another message or to try to phone her again even though he'd caught himself countless times, grabbing his phone, wanting to share something with her. He had this ridiculous idea that after a few days he'd have forgotten all about her. As if anyone could ever forget Charlie once they'd met her. Just another thing this week that hadn't worked out as planned.

A few minutes later, he jumped up, scowling and cursing a blue streak. Damn interfering woman! Anna had scheduled his first meeting for seven o'clock, damn it to hell. She knew how he hated those very early meetings. And she'd cleared his calendar for the rest of the day. There it was in black and white—he had an appointment with Charlie Wilson, Bowen therapist in Alisson at four o'clock.

His phone rang. It was his mother. For a minute, he considered throwing his phone against the wall. The trouble of replacing it would be considerably easier than having to deal her.

"Mom." He was curt and rude but at this point he didn't care. Why the hell was everyone suddenly interfering in his life?

"Oh, dear. It's your I'm-the-boss voice. What's wrong?"

"Nothing's wrong. Why are you phoning?"

"Can't I just phone my son?"

Exasperated, he rubbed his face. "Yes, Mom, of course you can."

"That's much better. I'm so happy you're coming home this weekend! That's why I'm phoning. It was so lovely to hear from Anna! We didn't see her the last time we were in Seattle. And I can't tell you what a relief it is to know your back is better. You are absolutely doing the right thing by returning for more sessions with the lovely Charlie. I'm so thrilled. I've bought all the ingredients today and will be cooking your favorite chicken pie tomorrow."

"Mom, please, no!" he finally managed to get a word in. His mother, bless her soul, was the worst cook, not that this technicality ever stopped her from trying.

"You don't like my cooking?"

"It's...not that," he managed. "Let me take you and Brooke out to dinner and—"

"Oooh, that sounds absolutely divine. A fabulous new restaurant has just opened. I'll book a table for us right away. Have a safe trip!" And before he could say goodbye, she'd put the phone down.

He sighed, realizing he'd been conned again. By his own mother. She'd probably made the booking already. He walked toward the big window. The view from here, over the city, was breathtaking, but today he barely noticed anything.

Charlie. She was all he thought about. He'd missed important details in the meeting that afternoon, all because he wasn't paying attention the whole time, a first for him.

He was going to see Charlie tomorrow. He'd be able to touch her, smell her. kiss her, hold her…

Swearing, he grabbed his jacket and car keys. What the hell was he thinking? It had been four whole days. He should've been over this damn crush by now, because a crush was all it could be. But here he was, dreaming about Charlie in broad daylight!

He should remember what she wore, her cluttered, colorful house, the countless bangles, for crying out loud. But as he drove home, all he could recall were her smile, the look in her eyes after he'd kissed her, the soft curve of her breasts, and her long, silky arms around his neck.

Swearing loudly, he sped home. And just before he turned into the block of apartments where he lived, he was finally able to give a name to the emotion in his chest—he was excited. He was going to see Charlie tomorrow and he was thrilled. Go figure. Resigned, he shook his head.

CHAPTER 9

Charlie checked her watch as she hurried home. It was nearly six o'clock. Lindsay had finished earlier that day, and when Gavin phoned to say he'd be arriving around five o'clock, her sister had taken the car so someone would be at home to welcome him.

She loved walking. There was a time, right after the accident in which her parents were killed, when she hadn't known whether she'd ever be able to walk again. But with Lindsay's encouragement and the help of a wonderful Bowen therapist, she'd beaten the odds and had found her true calling.

As a nursing sister, she'd seen so many people struggling with pain and after she'd discovered the many ways in which the Bowen technique helped relieve pain, she'd known that this was what she'd wanted to do with the rest of her life.

It was another gorgeous summer's day, and smiling, Charlie inhaled the fresh air. After sunny South Africa, the harsh long and cold Montana winters were something she and Lindsay struggled with at first. Although they've learned to embrace the joys of winter, she always looked forward to summer.

She loved the long, gentle days—they reminded her of the simpler times of their childhood—when their parents were still alive, before abusive boyfriends and big decisions changed their lives forever.

As she briskly walked home, she encountered several people along the way who were either running or walking. Some wanted to chat; others waved while continuing their exercise.

When she and Lindsay had arrived here two years before, the town's people hadn't immediately accepted the two strangers in their midst, but slowly and with Eleanor and Brooke's help, they now finally felt as if they belonged here. They were happy.

But now, within the span of a few days, their peaceful new life had been thrown into turmoil. Although Lindsay hadn't heard anything again from her ex-boyfriend, she was on edge. The telltale dark circles under her eyes confirmed she wasn't sleeping properly, and she never quite relaxed—her eyes kept darting around.

And then there was Logan. After Saturday night's messages, she hadn't heard from him again, but to her utter dismay, she'd caught herself checking her phone every so often. It was driving her crazy.

She'd been trying all week to understand why someone so completely unsuited for her would fill her mind and thoughts to such an extent she hardly slept, she had no appetite and—and this was the pits—she missed him. How could that be possible? She'd seen him four times. Four. Okay, each encounter had been...exceptional, but still. Pining for a man was so not something she wanted to be doing.

Still deep in thought, she turned to walk down the street where she and Lindsay lived. Something cold touched her spine. She stopped. Something was wrong. A strange uneasiness settled in her gut. Quickly she glanced up and down the street.

It was quiet. There was no movement and she couldn't

see anything out of the ordinary except… A small white car was parked on the opposite side of where she was walking. It didn't belong to anyone living in the street. It didn't look as if there was anyone in the car, but the windows were dark, so it was difficult to be sure.

Quickly, she crossed the street. As she neared the car, however, it started and before she could reach it, it sped away. Startled, she stared after the car. Who would…? Cold fingers clutched her throat. Mark Taylor? She wouldn't put anything beyond that horrible man.

Looking over her shoulder, she hastened home. She was so glad Gavin was here, and hopefully he could help her persuade Lindsay to continue with the self-defense classes. For some or other reason, her sister was very adamant about not going back, but hopefully after she'd heard about this incident, she'd realize how necessary it was for her to continue to learn to defend herself. What a dreadful notion, though, that it was necessary to learn to defend oneself against a man.

Why did men hurt women? Not always with violence, but also with words. Mark's abusive language had nearly destroyed Lindsay's self-image, and the way Toby had dismissed Charlie because she couldn't give him kids was hurtful, even now. He'd been so nice, initially. His true colors had only been revealed when he'd discovered she couldn't fall pregnant.

The front door opened as she neared the house and there was Gavin. She laughed, and opening her arms, she ran toward her brother. Her brother was one of the good guys. Like their dad, he was a caretaker and a nurturer. Next time she fell for someone, she was going to make sure she picked a man like him.

He hugged her tightly against him and for a moment she inhaled his familiar aftershave. "I'm so, so glad you're here." She sighed and gave him another hug before she smiled up at him.

But he knew her too well. "What happened?"

Lindsay appeared in the hallway behind Gavin.

"Let's go inside, and I'll tell you about it. But I think we all need a glass of wine."

"I've made lasagna, Gavin's favorite," Lindsay said, turning away but not before Charlie noticed the worried frown.

Charlie ached for her sister. Maybe she shouldn't tell Lindsay about the car she'd seen. But she quickly dismissed the thought. Her sister needed to know what was going on. Maybe then she'd consider continuing with the classes.

"Great. Gav—will you pour the wine, please? Take a seat when you're done; I'll quickly make a salad."

Gavin poured the wine and soon they were sitting around the table, enjoying Lindsay's lasagna.

"Okay, so why were you freaked out when you got home?" Gavin asked.

Charlie put her hand on her sister's arm. "I'm not quite sure what I've seen, but yeah, I think I'm a little freaked out." She told them about the white car in the street.

"But maybe it's nothing," Charlie added quickly when Lindsay inhaled sharply. "It could be an innocent visitor who was taking a drive around the village—it happens."

"But you don't think so?"

"I'm not sure…" Before she could complete her sentence, the doorbell rang. Charlie looked at Lindsay. "You're expecting anyone?"

Lindsay shook her head. "It could be Brooke or Eleanor…"

"It would be lovely to see them." Charlie smiled. "Gav, get more glasses; they're probably here to check you out."

"Who's Brooke and Eleanor?" Charlie heard him ask Lindsay as she quickly walked to the front door.

It was indeed their two friends and little Connor. Brooke had a bottle of wine in one hand. "Mom insisted on coming to meet your brother." She grimaced.

"Come in, come in. We're still eating, but there's more

than enough for you, as well." She bent down to the little boy. "I'm so glad you've come to visit. Come say hi to Lindsay."

"You still have the cars I can play with?" the little boy asked as they walked back to the kitchen.

"Yes, of course I have; they've been waiting for you. Let me get them for you." She pointed toward Gavin. "This is my brother Gavin. Gavin, meet Connor."

Gavin stood up before he extended his hand. "It's good to meet you, Connor."

After hesitating for a second, the little boy put out his hand. "My daddy died," he said.

Brooke gasped. "Connor…"

Gavin looked solemnly at the little boy while they shook hands. "I'm sorry. That hurts, doesn't it? My daddy also died."

Connor stepped forward and put his arms around Gavin's legs. A little awkwardly, Gavin patted his back.

"Gavin," Lindsay said, "this is Connor's mom, Brooke, and his grandma, Eleanor."

Gavin bent and picked Connor up before he extended his hand. "Lindsay has just been telling me how you helped them when they arrived here."

But Eleanor ignored his hand. She rushed forward and embraced him. "It's wonderful to meet you! We're so glad you were able to visit now."

"Mommy, you should also hug Gavin," Connor demanded, his one arm placed around Gavin's shoulders.

Everyone laughed while Brooke stepped forward and gave Gavin a quick hug.

Lindsay brought extra plates, Gavin poured more wine, and Charlie found the box of old toys she kept when friends with kids visited. They'd barely begun to eat when the doorbell rang again.

Lindsay's eye's widened, and Charlie put her hand on her sister's shoulder as she got up. "He's too much of a wimp to knock on our door, relax." Quickly, she walked to the front door and opened it.

"Hi, Charlie." It was Blake Davidson, the martial arts instructor.

"Blake?" Charlie got out, surprised and a bit wary to see him. Why was he here?

"You and Lindsay weren't at the dojo tonight. I...uhm, I wanted to check whether everything is okay? I believe there have been some trouble. Eleanor mentioned—"

"Blake!" Eleanor called out from behind Charlie. "Come on in—I'm sure there is more than enough food for you as well."

Charlie's suspicion evaporated, and she smiled. If Eleanor didn't find it strange that Blake had knocked on their door, then it was okay. "Come on in," Charlie said, much friendlier than before.

"Oh, but I didn't..." he began, but Eleanor pulled him inside and closed the door.

"Come on, you can try and persuade Lindsay to continue with your classes." Charlie uttered the last words as they entered the kitchen again.

"Gavin, meet Blake, the new martial arts instructor in town. Lindsay, explain to him why you don't want to continue with his classes. Blake, there's an empty chair next to Lindsay," she motioned. "Wine?" she asked as he sat down.

"Thank you, yes. But let me help?"

"It's fine." Charlie smiled, glancing at Lindsay, who had had gone very quiet since Blake's arrival.

Connor had been playing on the carpet, but with a car clutched in each hand, he approached the table again, his eyes on Blake. "Who's the man, Mommy?"

Blake got up and crouched down in front of Connor. "I'm Blake. I'm new in town."

"I'm Connor."

Blake also shook the little boy's hand and Charlie quickly glanced at Lindsay. Growing up, they were used to gentle, caring men. And of course, initially, that was the only side of Mark they'd seen when Lindsay had introduced him to her for the first time. It had only been afterward that he'd gradually started chipping away at her self-confidence until she'd lost every ounce of her self-esteem.

Gavin waited until Connor was playing with the cars again before he cleared his throat. "I assume you all know about the threatening message Lindsay received from her psycho ex-boyfriend last Friday?"

"Gavin, no, please…" Lindsay interrupted.

"I've told Blake what has happened," Eleanor said. "This is a small town and we all look out for each other."

Gavin stretched out his hand and patted Lindsay's arm. "The more people know what's going on, the better. This is not something you should be ashamed of, sis. You did absolutely nothing wrong."

Charlie hugged her sister. "Gavin is right, Linds. It makes sense to tell our friends so that everyone can be on the lookout."

Blake held up his hands and turned to Lindsay. "I don't think I fall under the category of friends…yet. Would you prefer it if I leave?"

Lindsay threw her hands in the air. "I seriously don't see why you'd be interested—"

"I'm…interested," Blake interrupted curtly.

Not even trying to hide her irritation, Lindsay sighed. "It's an ex-boyfriend from South Africa. He…didn't like it when I broke it off."

"And he's an abusive son of a—" Gavin began heatedly.

Lindsay put her hand on his arm to stop his rant.

"The message you've received—it was from him?" Blake asked her.

Lindsay nodded.

"And then tonight," Gavin said, "Charlie saw a strange car on this street. When she approached it, it sped away quickly."

"But I don't know if it was Mark," Charlie added quickly, worried about Lindsay's pallor.

Eleanor, bless her heart, lifted her glass. "Let's talk about happy things. I've booked a table at the new restaurant for us for tomorrow evening and I'm hoping you'll all join us?"

Brooke raised her eyebrows. "What a lovely idea, Mom."

Charlie turned to ask Lindsay what she thought, but her sister and Blake were in a heated, whispered discussion. Before she could ask Lindsay if she was happy to go to dinner the following evening, Blake stood up. "Thanks for the wine, and dinner. I have to go."

"I hope you'll join us tomorrow evening?"

He shook his head, glancing at Lindsay. "Maybe another time. Good night, everyone."

Lindsay ignored him and began to clear the table. Mmm, something strange was going on here; usually Lindsay got along with everybody.

"Thanks for stopping by." Charlie followed Blake to the front door.

On the porch, he turned around. "Please see if you can't convince your sister to return to the self-defense classes? And do let me know if she...if any of you need help? I have contacts ... there are people who can help."

"Thanks, will do." Charlie smiled and waved as he ran down the steps toward his car.

Blake had contacts? What contacts? She glanced up and down the street. There weren't any strange cars in sight, thank goodness.

Closing the door, she gnashed her teeth. Nothing was going to happen to Lindsay while she was around.

CHAPTER 10

When Logan parked in front of Charlie's rooms on Friday afternoon, he was fifteen minutes late. He glanced at his watch, then swore. This was what happened when women took over your life.

He should've been in his office working, yet here he was, waiting to see Charlie. Just about panting, to be honest. The flight had been slightly delayed; it took time to get a car and then he'd driven way too fast to get here. Why? Because he wanted to see Charlie. He needed to see her with a near desperation that was really scary.

For a moment he just sat in his car, breathing. Inside was Charlie. The reason why he couldn't sleep or eat or concentrate on his work. The reason he'd left work, traveled the distance to Alisson again in less than a week.

Cursing, he got out and strode toward the building. It had been six days since he'd first seen her. Maybe this craziness had run its course; maybe, by some miracle, when he'd see her again in a few minutes, she'd just be another pretty girl he'd kissed one night.

The bubbly receptionist he remembered from a week ago was chatting on the phone when he entered. Her eyes widened when she saw him and she quickly ended her call.

"Good day, Mr. Johnson." She smiled and stepped out from behind the counter. "We didn't know you're the four o'clock! Please follow me. Charlie will be so…surprised." She chuckled.

He clenched his teeth. Bloody Anna. So, she'd never mentioned his name to Charlie? It was high time he fired her; this was getting ridiculous.

The receptionist threw open Charlie's door. "Charlie— do I have a surprise for you!" she called out while motioning him to enter. "I'll see you Monday," she sang. "Lindsay has already left for the day. I'll lock the front door on my way out!" And then she was gone.

Somewhere in his befuddled brain this important piece of information registered—he and Charlie were all alone for the rest of the day.

And there she was, standing behind her chair, looking breathtakingly beautiful. A soft, polka-dot dress, the color of watermelon, crossed snugly over her breasts. And if he wasn't mistaken, one solitary button was all that kept the dress in place. Her bangles jingled as if they were nervous; the shining mini-chandeliers on her ears swung from side to side as she moved.

Without taking his eyes off her, he walked into the room and closed the door behind him.

He now accepted what he hadn't wanted to acknowledge all week long—it was going to take a while before he could get Charlie out of his thoughts, his dreams, his mind. She was never going to be just another girl he'd kissed.

To forget about Charlie wouldn't be easy.

All the blood left her brain, and for a moment Charlie was worried she was going to pass out like an old-fashioned love story heroine. She leaned against the wall, waiting for life to return to her feet.

She hadn't expected to see Logan ever again. Yet here

he was, another perfectly knotted tie around his neck, buttoned-up jacket, hair neatly combed backward. How she would love to mess up all that perfectly groomed hair. For a moment, she was worried she'd spoken out loud.

He was coming closer and closer. She couldn't breathe. For heaven's sake, she needed to remember what he'd said: she wasn't his type. Replaying the words over and over in her head like a mantra, she watched as he walked around her desk until he stood directly in front her.

"Charlie."

Her breath got stuck in her throat, but she nevertheless opened her mouth, hoping she would at least sound as if seeing him hadn't just sent her heartbeat into a frenzy. "Logan." Surely the husky, sexy voice wasn't hers?

"Where do you want me?" he asked, his eyes on her mouth.

What was he talking about? She'd take him anywhere and anytime...

"On the table?" he asked, turned around, and walked toward it. "On my back or face down?"

Of course, he was talking about the table—what was she thinking? Finally, she got her voice back and her feet miraculously moved. "Face down, please? I'll be with you in a minute."

And she nearly ran out of the room. Out of breath, she reached the bathroom. Inhaling deeply, she washed her hands and stared at herself in the mirror. She could do this. It was only forty-five minutes. What could happen in forty-five minutes?

Focusing on her breathing, she tried to get her heart to settle down, but by the time she walked back into the room, her hands were still shaking so much, she wasn't sure whether she'd be able to help Logan.

She fidgeted with her bangles while walking toward the table, and it was only when she'd reached it that she looked up. He was lying face down all right, but this time he'd not only taken off his jacket and tie, he'd also taken

83

off his shirt.

He heart kicked against her ribs. "It wasn't... You didn't have to..." she began, but again she sounded more call girl than professional therapist, and she swallowed the rest of her questions. This was a job. He was a client. In pain. And she could help.

"It's more comfortable this way." His voice was gruff.

She cleared her throat. "So, do you still experience some discomfort?" she got out. "Exactly where?" Oh, my goodness, that came out very wrong.

He turned his head and opened his eyes. "You really want to know?"

She shivered and shook her head. Was it her imagination or had the temperature in the room risen several degrees? From the previous times she'd done this, she knew exactly where on his back she should apply the rolling movements, but she hesitated. Today, there wasn't a shirt between her hands and his body. She'd be touching him without any barrier between flesh and flesh.

Taking a deep breath, she put her hands on him and tried to focus on the gentle massaging technique she knew so well. She didn't have to get palpitations simply because she was touching a man, for crying out loud.

"Talk to me?" he asked. "Tell me something. Anything. Because otherwise I may just get up and do something we'll both regret." He inhaled deeply. "Tell me more about this...this therapy."

How was she supposed to talk when her blood was pounding, her heart just about jumping out of her body, her breasts swollen in anticipation, her body getting ready for...? Oh, help! She was burning up.

Talk. Good idea. She could talk. She loved talking. Usually when working with clients, she was unfazed and would chatter away, trying to get her clients to relax, but with this guy there was no way she could relax. Every cell in her body was on red alert, as if waiting for something.

Doing her level best to ignore the haze of lust

threatening to engulf her, she began the rolling motions on the soft tissue of his lower back, while answering his question.

She'd told the story often enough; by this time, she knew it by heart. "It …" Oh, my word, what was up with her voice? Clearing her throat, she continued, "It was developed by Thomas A. Bowen in the 1950s. He lived in Geelong, Australia, and after serving in World War II, he became interested in finding out ways to relieve pain in the human body. Apparently, he loved sports and it was while attending games, Victorian-rules football games, he became interested in massage and other soft-tissue manipulation."

"So, where did you hear about the technique?"

"My back… I was in a car accident and had a problem for a while. Doctors wanted to operate but I wasn't keen. I tried other therapies, but nothing worked. Someone told me about the Bowen technique and although I was very skeptical at first, I thought I'd give it a try. After four visits, I was fed up and cancelled the rest of my sessions. But the very next morning I woke up without pain."

"And here we are," he said.

She lifted her hands. "And here we are," she repeated. "Okay, relax, I'll be back in a little while."

But before she could move, in one movement, he'd rolled over and was sitting on the bed. Her gaze was level with his chest, and although her brain was sending her frantic messages to leave, her feet refused to cooperate. She zoomed in on his muscled torso, also ignoring the alarm bells.

A perfect six-pack. Of course, he'd have a perfect six-pack; everything about him was perfect.

"Charlie." His voice was guttural, sending her already overstimulated senses into a frenzy. Warm fingers slid around her neck; he lifted her chin. His blue eyes had darkened, with desire. "I'm going to kiss you. It's all I've been thinking of all week…"

Slowly, he pulled her closer. Hypnotized, she stared at his mouth. He was giving her ample opportunity to stop him, but she wasn't going to. He knew that. She knew that. Because finally, she could admit to herself how much she wanted this; she'd been dreaming about this for nearly a week.

The roaring in his ears eliminated all other sounds. Nothing else mattered but to quench this thirst and satiate the hunger deep inside of him, something he could now acknowledge, was only possible here, with her.

Finally, his lips found hers. Soft. Welcoming. Wet. He could spend days, hours, simply kissing her. His arms gathered her closer. Roses and satin and curves and sexy lines—all woman. Finally, he was able to do what he'd been dreaming about for days—touch her.

Joyously, his tongue found its way to where it tangled with hers in a slow, sexy dance. Swallowing her gasp, he opened his legs wider, pulling her closer, making sure she knew exactly what being near her did to him. And still it wasn't enough. Not even close.

Desperately, as he slipped his hand beneath the V of her dress, he was intent on one thing only—to touch her softness. Maybe then he would be able to rein in this galloping desire to devour her. But the minute he encountered her hardened nipple, his heart tripped, slid into another gear.

He lifted his head. Glazed blue eyes stared up at him.

"I have to..." he whispered, and trailing his mouth over her chin, down her neck, he undid the button. He was right—it was the only thing keeping the dress in place.

It was a good thing he was sitting down. Otherwise he probably would've keeled over at the sight before him. Black satin and lace. That was all she was wearing underneath the dress. Black against pearl-white skin.

"You're killing me," he groaned and watched as her

eyes fluttered open.

With his eyes never leaving hers, he covered her breasts with both his shaking hands. "Beautiful, so beautiful," he whispered. "Do you have any idea what you're doing to me?"

He bent down, desperate to have more of her. His hands slipped the dress over her shoulders, and with a whisper, it dropped to the ground.

"Logan," she gasped. Her fingers spread out over his chest, sending his blood pounding through his veins. He tried to unhook her bra—he was usually quite adept at it—but this time he was clumsy, struggling to complete the simple task.

With a swift movement, she helped him. Generous breasts spilled out into his eager hands. He claimed her lips again, his hands kneading, worshiping, reveling in the softness of her curves.

And still he wanted more.

He lifted his head, drinking in the sight of her, only dressed in those damn bangles, mini-chandeliers on her ears, and a small triangle of black silk and lace.

With his eyes never leaving hers, he skimmed his hands down the sides of her body. She shuddered and with a groan, he gathered her close. He was ready to burst, but all he could think about was pleasuring the woman in his arms.

Unsteadily, his hand slipped down her body so that he could finally touch her intimately.

Charlie was burning up. Around them the air had thickened, making breathing difficult. Clever fingers explored and stroked and rubbed, and she was lost. Her whole body began to tremble. Her head fell backward while one delicious tremor after another took her to a place she'd never been before.

When she was finally able to focus again, Logan had

reversed their positions. She was now sitting on the bed and he was standing in front of her, his arms around her.

"That..." He exhaled. "That was beautiful."

He claimed her lips again, her hands slid slowly over down his back, and... Gasping, she lifted her head and looked down. He was gloriously naked. Her heart kicked against her ribs, heating her blood instantly. All muscles and toned lines, he was magnificent.

"Like what you see?" he asked, his voice husky.

Talking wasn't possible—she could only nod. Eagerly, her hands closed around him. Velvet heat throbbed in her hand, nearly sending her over the edge again.

With a groan, he caught her hands. "If you do that, this will be over way too soon and I want... I need to be inside you."

He pulled her closer but then stopped and cursed softly. "Damn, I nearly forgot. Protection. My pants."

Moments later, he claimed her mouth again.

A whirlwind of feelings mixed with passion and something she couldn't quite put a name to swept her up. Unable to communicate these intense feelings, she simply clung to him.

Big, warm hands stroked her body, lighting little fires just beneath her skin everywhere they went. Hungrily, his mouth scraped and nibbled her flesh, the sensation of his lips and tongue torturing her.

Frantically, she reared up, skimming her nails down his back, demanding more. The ache in her belly was unbearable, his body the only panacea. She was shivering—from heat, from need, from desire. "Logan..." she managed, dragging his head closer so their lips could meet again.

His mouth was hot and urgent and she nearly came apart right then. Without lifting his lips from hers, he spread her legs wider and with one forward thrust of his body, he slid into her.

She closed around him like a glove, choking out his name, and he almost lost control. This was home—here, inside of her, being a part of her.

He tried to slow down—this was for her—but his muscles quivered in protest. He'd never wanted anyone with such a hunger; he'd never wanted to please anyone else this much.

Her body curved up, her head fell back, and she cried out as she hit the next crest. A red haze threatened to blur his vision, but he desperately tried to focus. He wanted to give her more, and he had to see her when they both exploded.

"Look at me," he got out.

Dazed, she stared at him, her face flushed, her eyes darkened with desire. Deep inside him something stirred, but she began to move, and within seconds, they'd reach the pinnacle together. With her name a mantra on his lips and the sound of her jingling bangles in his ears, he threw back his head and took them both over the edge.

CHAPTER 11

Exactly how it happened, she wasn't sure, but they were both lying on the narrow table when she became aware of her surroundings again. Logan was behind her, his hands on her breasts, their legs entangled.

"I can't believe we're both on this table." She giggled and lifted her hand to touch his face.

His laugh rumbled in her ear and he hugged her close. "My leg is numb, but I'm not complaining."

Her phone rang. She tried to move, but he held her closer still. "One more minute, please?"

"It may be Lindsay," she said. "And I don't want her to worry."

He let her go and she got up.

"Why would she worry? Have you heard from the ex-boyfriend again?"

But it was very difficult to answer questions when he was still buck naked. And look at his hair—she'd messed it up all right. There were things she should be doing. Putting on her clothes, phoning Lindsay…

"How the hell am I supposed to get dressed if you look at me like that?" he murmured, and with two strides, he reached her. Burying his face in her neck, he pulled her close. "I don't think I'll ever get enough of you."

He was ready for her again. Oh, my. Hungry lips claimed hers and she was lost.

Another hour passed before they were finally dressed. Charlie was on the phone with Lindsay while he locked the door to their rooms. If he'd had his way, they would've stayed here for the rest of the night. But besides the fact that the table was really uncomfortable and definitely not meant for making love, Logan knew his mother was waiting for him.

"Can I give you a ride home?" he asked.

"Please, if you don't mind. I love walking home, but it's now so late after you...after we..." Her cheeks reddened and he smiled.

"I can't believe you're still blushing after I've ravished you for the past two hours," he teased, taking her hand.

Her breath hitched. "Don't say things like that; we'll never leave here if you do."

"And what you're saying will help?" he growled, then kissed her.

She giggled and danced around to the passenger seat, bangles jingling, earrings bouncing. Laughing, he followed her and opened the door. As she climbed into the car, one long, sexy leg flashed between the panels of her dress for a moment before she demurely closed it.

"Damn woman, you're killing me." He bent down and kissed her, his hand quickly finding its way through the slip of the dress to her heat. "How the hell am I supposed to keep my eyes on the road," he murmured against her lips.

Her eyes darkened and she grabbed his hand. "Logan..."

Cursing, he moved, bumped his head against the roof of the car, and cursed again.

She giggled. "Poor baby."

She was still chuckling when he started the car. "You

think this is funny?" He reached for her hand. "Feel what you do to me." He pressed her hand against his crotch. Her breath hitched and she leaned in for a quick kiss.

"Now behave," she admonished, folding her hands primly on her lap.

But he simply had to take her hand again while he was driving. He glanced at her, and that was all it took for his body to react to her again. He was like a sex-starved schoolboy. Surely, he could talk about normal things and not only think about the next time he could have her again?

Talk. Yes. They'd been distracted earlier. He turned into the street where she lived. "You haven't answered my question yet. Has Lindsay heard from her ex-boyfriend again?"

Charlie shook her head. "No. But I..." She caught her bottom lip between her teeth while she turned around in her seat and glanced over her shoulder.

"What?" he asked as he parked in front of her house.

"I don't know. Maybe it was nothing; maybe..."

Really upset now, he scowled. "Charlie, damn it, what happened?" Just the thought that something might be troubling her upset him.

"I was walking home last night when I saw a car parked here in this street, close to our house. It's not a car I've seen here before and it quickly sped away when I approached it, but it doesn't necessarily mean anything."

"But you're worried."

"We're...more on edge, I'd say."

"Will you please let me know if anything happens that worries you or bothers you? The county sheriff and I went to school together. I've spoken to him about the message Lindsay's received. I'll tell him about this, as well."

"You really don't have to..."

He grabbed her hand and kissed her fingers. "Of course I do. If anything happened to you..." Not a sentence he wanted to finish.

Smiling, she softly touched his face. "Underneath the tie and suit, you're a nice guy, Logan Johnson. Thanks for the ride."

"Will you join my family and me for dinner tonight?" he asked.

She grinned cheekily. "Sorry, I already have a date."

Completely taken aback, he frowned. He hadn't even considered the possibility that she might have another man in her life. "Oh. Okay."

Angry and upset, he quickly got out and opened the door for her. She'd spent the afternoon with him, but she was going with some other man on a date? So the mind-blowing lovemaking just now was just another item on her Friday agenda?

Here he was, ready to throw her over his shoulder and take her far away so that they could be together—uninterrupted—but she had another date.

"Logan…" she began.

"No need to explain. Goodbye." And without looking back, he drove away.

The damn man was going to pay for behaving like a spoilt brat. Charlie combed her hair back with her fingers. She was still so mad, she hoped Logan's tongue would drop to the floor when he saw her. Dressing to look sexy had never been a goal for her, but tonight all she could think about was bringing Logan to his knees.

She, Gavin, and Lindsay had arrived at the restaurant minutes before. Earlier that afternoon, she'd only been teasing Logan. She was going to explain that his mother had already invited them, but by that time he'd already gotten all haughty and angry. The imbecile. He should know…after that afternoon…he should know she'd rather be with him than with anyone else.

Gavin parked in front of the restaurant. "I'm impressed," he said as they all got out. "This looks very nice."

Lindsay grabbed Gavin's arm and grinned at Charlie. "Alisson is a growing town, dear brother. Charlie, we have ourselves a very attractive man tonight; let's go make everyone jealous."

"And you gals look great, as well." Gavin smiled.

"Charlie is looking particularly sexy tonight. I wonder why?" Lindsay teased.

Before they'd reached the front door of the restaurant, someone called out their names. Alarmed, Lindsay looked around quickly, but her frown quickly turned into a smile. "It's Eleanor and Brooke. And of course, Logan."

Charlie turned around and there he was. Handsome as sin and with a glint in his eye. Ah. He'd finally figured out who her date was.

"Logan, you haven't met our brother yet," Lindsay said. "Gavin, this is Eleanor's son, Logan. Logan, our brother, Gavin."

The two men shook hands and Logan grimaced.

"Gavin, seriously," Charlie scowled. Her brother was always testing the men around his sisters by nearly crushing their hands.

And then Logan was beside her. "So this is your date? And you didn't think to tell me?" he said under his breath, his eyes raking over her.

Lifting her chin, she looked away. "You didn't give me a chance to explain."

The rest of the party were entering the restaurant. Grinning, Lindsay glanced at them. "I suppose you need a few minutes to talk to Charlie about…your back?"

Before Charlie could say anything, Logan had her by the elbow. "Yes, I do. Five minutes." Without waiting for Lindsay to reply, he steered Charlie to the side of the building where they couldn't be seen from the street.

"Logan, really…"

But before she could complete her sentence, his mouth was on hers and she forgot what she wanted to say. His hands swept down her sides before he cupped her breasts. Against her body, she felt his growing desire and her knees buckled. This man could turn her to mush simply by touching her.

Gulping in fresh air, he cupped her face. "I was an idiot. But the idea that you'd go on a date with someone else after this afternoon... I lose all logic when I'm near you." He groaned. "Look at you—you're beautiful, sexy, exquisite. How the hell am I supposed to keep my hands to myself?"

"You don't approve of what I wear, remember?"

He frowned, tracing the line of the off-the-shoulder shimmering blue top she was wearing. "But I do I love it when your shoulders are bare and I..." He touched her earrings with his one hand while the other one slipped below her top to cup her breast. "I dream about these damn mini-chandeliers."

"Mini-chandeliers? Seriously?" Her giggle turned into a gasp. He was fondling her breast; thinking was fast becoming impossible.

"Charlie! Logan! Where are you guys? We want to order!" Eleanor called from close by.

Swearing, Logan dropped his hands. "I have to...give me a minute."

Combing her unsteady fingers through her hair, Charlie inhaled deeply. "I'll see you inside."

Fortunately, Eleanor was not waiting for her, so she could slip into the bathroom. She definitely needed a minute, as well. Her heart was beating out of control. She sagged against the wall. How was she supposed to resist him?

Her legs were rubbery, the stupid butterflies frantic, and her whole body was aflame. How she was going to sit and eat and talk about ordinary things as if nothing had happened, she had no idea.

When Logan finally reached the table, Charlie was pulling out a chair. He stepped closer. "Let me?" he asked softly, and felt her shiver before she sat down. He sat down next to her, moving his chair slightly so that he could easily touch her.

"Well, isn't this lovely?" Eleanor beamed.

Logan caught the waiter's eye. He needed a drink. The blood was still roaring in his ears. Damn, this woman was killing him. He'd been livid when he'd left her earlier that afternoon, thinking she'd made a date with someone else. It was only after they'd parked in front of the restaurant that his mother had casually mentioned that the Wilsons would be joining them.

Charlie had wanted to explain; he hadn't given her a chance. He'd been so quick to jump to the wrong conclusion. Why? He glanced sideways at Charlie. She was laughing at something her brother was saying to her, and again he felt the strange shift inside of him.

"...heard anything about the car parked in your street?" Brooke's voice penetrated his thoughts.

Charlie had mentioned it earlier but he'd been so upset about the thought she'd be with someone else, he hadn't given the strange car another thought. He'd only been thinking of ways to get them alone again—damn it, he was completely out of control around her.

"I don't know," Lindsay said. "I haven't heard from him again—"

"But you are still taking the self-defense classes?' his mother interrupted her.

"Well..." Lindsay shifted uncomfortably in her chair. "I don't know if that will necessarily help. And ..."

"Am I too late?" someone asked and when Logan turned his head, there was the damn martial arts instructor, as well. What the hell?

But his mother was all smiles. "Blake! I'm so happy you could make it. Do sit down. I'm so glad I was able to change your mind. We're just talking about your self-defense classes. How are things going in the new dojo?"

The only available chair was next to Lindsay, and Blake pulled it out while he nodded to everyone around the table. "It's a slow start, but we'll get there," he said.

Charlie leaned forward. "Hello, Blake. Now is your chance to try persuade Lindsay she needs to continue with your classes."

"I'm fine," Lindsay said crossly.

Just then the waiter approached their table. "I'm sorry, I'm looking for Lindsay Wilson," he said.

"Why?" Gavin asked, getting up.

"There's a phone call for her." The waiter pointed in the direction of the entrance.

Lindsay paled visibly.

Charlie got up quickly. "I'll take the call, Linds."

"Follow me," the waiter said and walked toward the entrance of the restaurant.

Before Logan could react, Gavin also got up and took Charlie's arm as they left.

Charlie was so angry; if she'd ever had the misfortune of seeing Mark-freaking-Taylor, again, she would throttle him. This could only be him. But how did he know they were here?

Gavin was standing close to her when she answered the phone. "Yes."

"Lindsay?" It was Mark's voice.

"Yes."

"I'm coming for you, bitch," he snarled before the line was disconnected.

Charlie shivered and put the phone back.

"Who was it?" Gavin asked.

"It was Mark."

"What did he say?" asked Logan.

Charlie turned around; Logan had also followed them.

"He's coming for her. He used a more colorful

description."

Gavin swore. "So if he called here, it means…"

"He's around." Charlie nodded. "He knows our movements. Or someone else is telling him where we are."

Logan took her hand. "I'll speak to the sheriff again and tell him about the car and the phone call. If this guy is in Alisson, they'll find him."

Gavin was staring at their clasped hands. "And this?" He glared at Logan. "If you mess with my sister, there'll be hell to pay," he growled.

Charlie placed a hand on his arm. "Down, boy." She smiled. "We're having fun. I'm not his type; he's told me."

"What the hell?" Gavin nearly bellowed. "And you let him touch you?"

Charlie took her brother's hand. "Relax. Neither of us wants anything more; we're both in this with eyes wide open. Come on, Lindsay will want to know who phoned."

Gavin relaxed slightly, but he was still glaring at Logan. "Are we going to tell her?"

Charlie nodded. "Yes, she may not know it yet, but she's strong. She can handle it. She has us."

CHAPTER 12

Lindsay sat staring at Charlie long after she'd finished telling everyone about the call. Logan watched her. Like Charlie, she was beautiful, but at the moment she looked fragile. For a minute he was worried she might faint. But then she squared her shoulders, and lifting her chin, she swore softly.

His mother grinned. "That's my girl. Look around this table, sweetheart. We're all here for you. Brooke and I know most of the people in this town and we'll spread the word. This guy is not going to get close to you if we can help it."

"He's stolen my joy before. I'm not going to let him do that again," Lindsay declared.

"So does this mean we can continue with Blake's classes?" Charlie asked.

"Yes, okay, I'll go back. But," and she glared at Blake, "you're not to keep using me for demonstrations. And I'm not standing in the front row."

Blake nodded. "Yes, ma'am."

"And don't ma'am me," she scolded. Pleased that the tension had been somewhat relieved, everyone laughed.

Their food arrived and the talking became more

general.

"Are you working tomorrow?" Logan asked Charlie under his breath. He hadn't planned on asking her, but sitting here, so close to her, he couldn't think about anything else other than trying to be with her again.

She turned and looked at him. "I have one client at ten but then I'm free for the day."

"Want to go with me to a cabin near a lake tomorrow? We'll be back on Sunday."

She quickly glanced at Lindsay. "I'm not sure if I want to leave Lindsay alone…"

"Your brother is here," he said, and put his hand on her knee underneath the tablecloth.

She inhaled softly. "You can't do that!"

"Watch me." He grinned and swept his hand up her leg to touch her intimately. He waited for her gasp before he brought his hand back up from under her dress.

"Logan," she scolded, her cheeks flaming.

"I need to be with you, Charlie. Without interruptions." She exhaled slowly. "I'll text you tonight."

By the time there was a knock on her front door at lunch the next day, Charlie was a wreck. She checked her watch. One o'clock on the dot. Logan was here to pick her up.

She shouldn't go with him; this whole thing had heartache written all over it. She was setting herself up to be hurt. Badly. Gavin's words of the night before had also been bothering her for the fast eight hours. Her brother was right—she shouldn't let someone who'd told her she wasn't his type even touch her, let alone go away with him.

But when it came to Logan Johnson, her brain seemed to stop functioning. Refusing him was not an option. This was all temporary; he'd made that perfectly clear right from the beginning. And she knew she was not what he really wanted and needed in a wife. Also something he'd been very honest about.

He might want her for the moment. Need her, he'd said. It wouldn't last: she knew that. But her whole being wanted to be with him; she wasn't going to miss this opportunity.

Picking up her overnight bag, she glanced around the room, making sure she'd taken everything.

Lindsay knocked and opened her door. "You ready? The sooner you leave with Lover Boy, the better. Our brother is just about foaming at the mouth."

"Aargh, there really is no need. I told him last night, I'm very much aware that this is short-lived. Nobody has to get so worked up about it."

"You sure about this?" Lindsay asked.

Combing her fingers through her hair, Charlie sighed. "I want to be with him, sis. It's that simple."

Lindsay stared at her for a few minutes before she smiled slowly. "Don't tell me… You're in love with him, aren't you?"

Charlie's breath hitched. "Don't be silly. I can't…I don't…of course I'm…" But that was exactly what had happened. Feeling numb, she stared at her sister. "I love him," she whispered. "How did that happen?"

"Oh, Charlie." Lindsay gave her a quick hug. "We sure pick 'em, don't we? So what are you going to do?"

Charlie shook her head slowly, her thoughts chaotic. "I can't go away with him. It was okay before I didn't know what this craziness inside me was, but now…" Pressing her fingers against her eyelids, she shook her head. "I can't go. And anyway, we have our life here. A home, peace— that's the only thing I want right now."

Lindsay frowned. "It's not your job to 'make a home' for me, Charlie. Why would you think you need to do that?"

"After everything you've been through…"

Lindsay gave her a quick hug. "You were there for me when I needed you and I know you'll always be there for me, no matter where you are. Please don't put your own life on hold for me. I'm a big girl."

Charlie swallowed a sob that was threatening to escape. "It'll break my heart when he leaves."

"So what do I tell Logan?"

"Tell him…or no, wait, I'll tell him myself," Charlie murmured. She put down the overnight bag and inhaled deeply before she brushed past her sister.

The moment he saw Charlie coming down the stairs, Logan knew something was wrong. She didn't quite look him in the eye.

"Gavin, can you give us a minute?"

Gavin stubbornly crossed his arms and leaned against the kitchen door.

"Please?" she asked her brother again. "I'm…not going with him."

A sharp sword pierced Logan's heart. Gavin smiled triumphantly and moved into the kitchen.

"What the hell, Charlie?" Logan got out when Gavin was out of earshot.

Charlie's eyes were swimming with tears. "I can't go with you."

"Can't or won't?"

"I'm not what you want, Logan. You know that."

He grabbed her hand and pulled her into the living room. "What happened between yesterday and today? Last night you were with me, I—"

"I've had time to think."

He cupped her face, his eyes taking in every beautiful thing about her. "I can make sure you don't think."

She turned her face into his hand. "I know. It'll be so easy. It won't last, we both know it and I…" One tear slipped down her cheek. "I thought I could be with you on a temporary basis, but I can't."

He frowned. There was a subtext here he wasn't

getting. "You told me you don't want to get married, so what…?"

She placed her hand on his chest. "That was before…" Swallowing, she shook her head. "Don't make this harder than it already is, please?"

"That was before what?"

"Logan, please, just leave it…"

"No!" Trying to calm himself, he took a deep breath. He was fighting here, exactly what for, he wasn't sure, but he if he left now without Charlie… It wasn't something he was ready to think about. "No," he said in a calmer voice. "Before what? What happened, damn it? Please tell me."

She dropped her hands. "Before I…fell for you."

"Fell for me?" His brain was struggling to make sense of the simple words.

She gave him a lopsided smile. "Yeah, I've gone and fallen in love with you. Even after you've told me I'm not your type. Your words hurt me so much—I should've known why—but I've only realized it now. And that's why I can't go away with you."

Dumbfounded, he stared at her. She'd fallen in love with him. That was what she'd just said. In love. With him.

"Goodbye, Logan," she whispered before she turned around and hurried out of the room.

"What have you done to my sister?" bellowed Gavin from the doorway.

Still stunned, Logan stared at the angry man and shook his head. "I haven't… She…" But he was unable to string more than two words together. A tight band had fastened around his chest and was squeezing all the oxygen out of his lungs. He had to get some fresh air. "Excuse me," he muttered, and quickly left.

He'd hurt her. She loved him. Loved him.

In his car, he texted his mother. He was going back to Seattle; there was a flight later that night. Space. He needed space and distance from this place to sort out his chaotic thoughts.

She couldn't cry. Dry-eyed, Charlie stared at the ceiling. She loved Logan. Deeply, irrevocably, passionately. Even though she'd known he would hurt her. Damn it, he did hurt her, telling her she wasn't his type, criticizing who she was, her clothes, her taste.

Within the span of eight days, she'd gone and lost her heart to a man who found fault with everything about her, but one who also made her feel things she hadn't known were possible.

Ecstasy. That was what she'd experienced. Drug-free. And the reason was because for her, what had happened between them, hadn't been just sex. She'd made love with him. With her body and hands and mouth, she'd told him how she felt, even though she hadn't known it herself before today.

She'd never had this instant attraction to anyone before, but with Logan...

Turning on her side, she closed her eyes, hugging the pillow close to her. She'd have to get over him. Somehow. Life happened, things went awry at times, as she very well knew.

Maybe someday, she'd be able to tell Lindsay or Gavin's kids about her one big love, the one who broke her heart.

And then the tears came. She buried her face in the pillow and sobbed her heart out. This falling-in-love business hurt, damn it.

Logan was still in shock when he opened the door to his apartment in Seattle much later that night. He dropped the keys onto the table next to the door and walked into his living room.

An interior decorator had put his ideas into practice, and the monochrome tones and clean lines had always soothed him when he got back home. But tonight the place looked bare. Cold. Lifeless. Charlie-less.

Minutes later, he was on the balcony, staring out over the city with a drink in his hand. She'd fallen in love with him. He was struggling to get his head around it. What the hell was love, anyway? Sex he understood, but love?

His parents had loved one another, he never doubted that. And Brooke and her husband had been seemingly happy before his untimely death, but that was the exception rather than the rule. Most of his colleagues or friends were either still single or divorced, and those who were still married made no secret of how unhappy they were. What kind of a life was that?

And why was he thinking about families—unhappy or otherwise? That was so not what he wanted in his life. Marriage meant messy—not something he'd ever considered.

Downing the glass, he walked back into the house. It was pure lust, that was all. He'd been in lust before—it would pass. His work kept him busy enough; marriage was not for him. He'd always known that.

He sent a message to let his mother know he was home. Within seconds she phoned. Damn it, he didn't want to talk to her now, but he knew his mother. There was no knowing what she'd do if he didn't answer a call from her.

"Mom, I've just sent you a message."

"I don't want a message; I want to talk to my son."

He sighed. "There is nothing to talk about."

"Of course, there is. One minute you and Charlie were going away to a cabin, and the next minute I get a message from you telling me you're on your way back to Seattle."

"Mom, seriously, it's really none of your business, you know that, right?"

"What have you done?"

Exasperated he groaned. "I haven't done anything, Mom. She...she...it simply didn't work out. We're too different."

"Of course you are. That's what all the great love stories have in common!"

"You read way too many love stories, Mom. I love you and Brooke dearly, but your lifestyles would drive me crazy within days and so would Charlie. She is…" He tried to think of something about her that bothered him but all he remembered was her laugh, the way her eyes darkened when they'd made love, and how perfectly she fitted against his body. "Well, she…doesn't… It just can't work."

"Are you trying to convince me or yourself? Because quite frankly, I don't think either of us are fooled."

"Good night, Mom. I'll talk to you soon." Ending the call, he walked toward the big windows overlooking the city.

Great love stories? Trust his mother to come up with a corny line. At the moment he was hurt and upset, but by this time next week, all the craziness would be over.

But much later, when he lay on his bed in the dark, his hand kept straying to the empty place beside him. Damn, he missed Charlie.

Swearing, he switched on the light and picked up his phone. This was going to end right now. He probably needed to get out more. Date, have sex. Hadn't he told himself that days ago? It was time to actually do something about it. He'd met a woman a couple of months ago at a friend's house. What was her name again? Mandy? Sandy? The kind of woman he usually dated. They'd have a drink, enjoy a meal, talk about general things, and maybe have sex afterward. No complications, no messy feelings, no emotion. Quickly, he scrolled down the names on his phone.

Charlie. Her name was suddenly right there. For a long moment his finger hovered over it. What would she do if he called her now? Damn it to hell, he had to forget about her. She loved him and he…well, he didn't want that. He'd already hurt her, she'd pointed out. It confirmed what he'd known all along—relationships were simply not something he was good at. Or wanted. Period.

Love and feelings were complications he could do without. Sex he could do. And there were plenty of women who were happy with that. There was no need to make everything so damn difficult.

He should remember what living with a free spirit meant—no rules, no boundaries, no order, no structure.

And in his line of work he needed structure and discipline, otherwise things wouldn't get done. That was why he preferred women who dressed in muted colors and clean lines.

Quickly he found the name he was looking for and within minutes he had a date two weeks from now. Weekdays were impossible, he rarely got home before midnight and this coming weekend couldn't work; he had several meetings scheduled.

Mandy. He tried to picture her, but a pair of clear blue eyes was preventing him from doing that.

Cursing, he switched off the light. Soon, he'd have forgotten all about Charlie's eyes. And the slope of her shoulders. And the jingling of those damn bangles.

His eyes closed. Roses. Why the hell was he smelling roses?

CHAPTER 13

Early Sunday morning, Charlie was wakened by a knock on her door. Probably Lindsay. Bleary-eyed, she raised herself on an elbow.

"Come on in," she called out groggily and Lindsay and Gavin entered her room. Gavin was carrying a tray with coffee.

"You okay?" Lindsay asked, and sat next to her on the bed. "Did you get any sleep?"

Charlie rubbed her face. "A bit." She held out her hands for a mug of coffee. "This smells so nice, thanks."

Gavin also sat on her bed. "I should've given that bastard—" he began vehemently, but Charlie placed a soothing hand on his arm.

"He didn't do anything wrong, Gavin. He was very honest about the fact that he wasn't looking for anything permanent and neither am I, as you know. I'm hurting, yes, but it'll pass. These things do. Have you decided when you're going back to South Africa?" she asked, hoping to change the subject.

Gavin's frown didn't quite clear but at least he answered her question. "In two weeks' time, maybe. I've wanted to talk to the two of you about this. I'm thinking of also moving here to Alisson."

Lindsay clapped her hands and hugged Gavin. "I was really hoping you'd fall in love with our little town. But what about your job back in South Africa?"

"Actually, even before you called about Mark Taylor's message, I was talking to my partners back in Johannesburg about the possibility of moving here and working from here. With today's technology it's possible. I've really missed you guys. Maybe at some point, I'll consider moving to a big city again and joining another firm. But for now, the peace and quiet of this little town has grown on me."

"Seattle in Washington state is a little over an hour's flight from Bozeman, so it's quite close by," Lindsay said. "Charlie has a meeting there in two weeks. I was going to join her, but when you arrived, I decided to stay here with you. But why don't we all go? Surely you can wait a little longer before you fly back to South Africa? We can all have a lovely dinner Friday night and while Charlie has her meeting Saturday morning, you and I can explore the city."

Charlie shook her head. "I don't think I want to go anymore."

But Lindsay was not going to change her mind. "You are not going to let Logan Johnson prevent you from doing something you've been excited about for months. It's a big city—the chances of meeting him are practically nil."

"It sounds great," said Gavin.

Lindsay jumped up. "Cool—I'm going to book a flight for you, as well, Gavin. I've booked an apartment with beds for five people, according to the ad, so I think there'll be somewhere for you to sleep." She just about danced out of the room.

Gavin shook his head. "It will be good for her to get away. You sure you'll be okay?"

"I'll get there." Charlie smiled. "I'm so glad you've decided to join us here. We've missed you so much.

112

But…but about you and Sarah? I thought you guys were serious?"

Shrugging, Gavin stood up. "So did I. She didn't."

"So what…?"

But Gavin clearly didn't want to talk about it. "It's over. That's all there is to it. Come on, lazybones, I'm making breakfast."

Relationships seemed to be hard for all three of them.

Charlie got out of bed.

On Monday morning, Charlie was in her rooms at eight o'clock. Her first appointment was at nine, but she needed to be alone. Lindsay and Gavin meant well, but they'd hovered around her all of the day before, and their worried glances were driving her up the wall.

She couldn't sleep, her appetite had disappeared altogether, and there was hole inside her she didn't know what to do with.

There was a knock on her door and Eleanor peeped in. "I was on my way to buy muffins when I saw your car parked out front. Mind if I come in?" By the time she'd finished talking, she was already in the room.

Charlie crossed her arms. Logan's mom was really the last person she wanted to see. It was difficult enough not to think constantly about him. And Eleanor would want to talk about the cancelled trip to the cabin, she knew that.

"I don't want to talk about it," she said before Eleanor could say another word.

"About what, dear?" Eleanor asked as she sat down on one of the chairs.

"You know what. Logan and I…we're too different, it can never work—it's obvious."

"Not to me, it isn't. I've never seen such an instant connection between people as I've seen between the two of you. You can't deny that. It's rare and special and not something that happens every day."

With a sigh, Charlie sat down behind her desk. There was a lump the size of a tennis ball in her throat, and Charlie had to swallow several times before she could answer. "I'm not denying it. But…some things are simply not meant to be."

"Oh, nonsense," Eleanor exclaimed. "Logan can't take his eyes off of you and you, my dear girl, you light up when you see him. I don't want you to make a dreadful mistake. Love comes knocking once in a lifetime, if we're lucky. And I—"

"I love him, Eleanor. Body, soul, the works. But…he doesn't feel the same way. That's why I couldn't go away with him. Don't be mad at him, please. He's been very honest about it right from the start. I'm not what he wants. Besides, I…I can't have children and Logan deserves a whole woman, someone who can give him everything he wants. Your son is a good man, Eleanor, just not for me."

Eleanor stared at her for several minutes before she got up. "Not being able to have your own children doesn't make you less of a woman. I'm not sure why you believe that lie, but it's not true. You don't ever turn your back on love, sweetie, don't you know that? You fight for it!"

Swallowing her tears, Charlie walked around the desk and gave her a hug. "It doesn't always work out in real life. So, tell me—what are our plans for this week?"

Fortunately, Eleanor was happy to talk about other things. "Brooke is working non-stop on a commissioned piece, so I'll probably help out in the evenings with Connor. But let's make a date for Friday. As you know by now, I can't really cook, but…"

Charlie smiled. "That sounds nice, thanks. Next weekend we're all going to Seattle. Bowen therapists from surrounding states have a meeting there on Saturday. I made contact with them when we arrived, but I've never attended any of their meetings before. Lindsay and Gavin are coming with me, I'm glad to say. I think it'll be good for Lindsay to get away."

"You'll enjoy Seattle; it's a beautiful city." She grimaced. "You know, if you and Logan were still together, he could've shown you around."

"I'll be busy and Lindsay and Gavin will find their way." Charlie held her breath. She really didn't want to talk about Logan any longer. It was too hard.

Fortunately, Eleanor didn't push her point. "When is Gavin going back?" she asked on her way out.

"I don't think I've told you yet, but he's decided to join us here. He'll initially work for the firm he's with in South Africa and will take things from there."

Eleanor's eyes widened. "That is wonderful news." She quickly hugged Charlie. "I have to go and tell Brooke."

Shaking her head, Charlie walked back into her rooms. Why would Brooke be interested in Gavin's whereabouts? But hopefully Eleanor now had a different topic to focus all her energy on and would leave Charlie be.

Lilly knocked on her door, announcing the first client of the day. Great. At least while she worked, the ache inside her subsided for a while.

Two weeks later, Logan was ready to climb the walls. It was Friday, fourteen days since he'd last seen Charlie. He should've forgotten her by now, damn it. But he was like a zombie. He struggled to focus on his work, and he couldn't even remember the last time he'd had a decent night's sleep.

Everyone in the office, including Anna, was giving him a wide berth. He was unreasonable, irritated, angry, frantic—all at the same time, all the time.

Damn it to hell. Why couldn't he get the woman out of his thoughts and dreams? At the oddest times, he'd remember her smile or hear the jingling of her bangles. He was making himself and everyone around him miserable, and he had no idea how to stop the ache inside of him.

Anna knocked on the door, her face expressionless—a

clear sign she was fed up with him. "I've made reservations at the Italian restaurant you like so much for tomorrow night."

Logan was staring at his screen. For the past hour, he'd been trying to get an email out, but because he kept thinking about Charlie, he'd hardly written more than a paragraph. "Reservations? What reservations?"

"According to your calendar, you have a date. With someone called Mandy."

He frowned. Mandy? Who the hell was Mandy? And then he remembered the call he'd made two weeks before. He'd had nothing but Charlie on his mind for the last two weeks; he'd clean forgotten he'd made a date.

"Oh, yes. I remember. Lovely woman," he mumbled, and stared at his screen again.

"Really? What does she look like?"

What does Charlie look like? His gaze was still on screen, but his thoughts were right back in Alisson—in Charlie's rooms, to be exact. "She's...beautiful. Wears weird clothes, she probably has a hundred bangles on each arm, you know, and she loves these mini-chandeliers on her ears..."

"Oh, really? Because the Mandy I thought you were taking on a date is rake-thin, wears only black, white, or gray, and she wouldn't be seen dead in bangles."

Logan looked up. "Mandy?"

Anna cocked her head. "You've just described Charlie Wilson, the Bowen therapist in Alisson, if I'm not mistaken?"

He opened his mouth to refute her observation but closed it again. There wasn't anything to say. "I have work to do."

"Of course you do," she said primly and left his office. But he'd seen the twinkle in her eye.

Damn interfering woman. Leaning back in his chair, he cursed. He was going to enjoy tonight, even if it killed him, damn it.

Anna had barely closed the door behind her when his phone rang. It was his sister. Okay, her, he could handle, but not his mother. Not today, not when he was feeling so...so...raw.

"Hi, Brooke," he greeted her. "I'm sure by now you've spoken to Mother. I'm fine. As a matter of fact, I have a date tonight. We're going to that nice Italian restaurant I've taken you guys to the last time you were here."

"A date? Really? That was quick, even for you." She sounded amused. "But that's not why I'm calling. I'm actually phoning to talk to you about my portfolio, if now is convenient?"

But he knew his sister. She didn't have to call about her investments. She received monthly reports and she'd know exactly what was going on. But okay, he'd play along. Sooner or later, he'd discover the real reason for her call. "Of course."

Quickly he opened her file on his computer and for a few minutes they discussed her funds. Then he closed the file and sat back in his chair. "Okay, so why did you really call?"

She laughed. "You know me too well. Okay. I was curious to know if you've already forgotten about Charlie. You never take your eyes off of her when she's around, did you know that? Anyway, now I know you've obviously moved on and are already dating other women. Such a pity, but we'll find Charlie a nice husband. There is this one rancher..."

And before he could react, she'd ended the call.

He quickly got up and started pacing. What damn rancher? The mere thought of Charlie with another man was driving him insane.

There was a knock on his door. He had a meeting. Work was supposed to take his mind off Charlie, damn it! Why the hell wasn't it working?

Late Saturday afternoon after a whole day spent talking everything Bowen, Charlie was tired, but exhilarated as an Uber dropped her off at the little cottage Lindsay had rented for them in Seattle. It had been a long day, but she'd enjoyed every minute of it. She'd met a group of enthusiastic and wonderful fellow Bowen therapists who were all very willing to help the newcomer in their midst.

The past two weeks had been exhausting. A thousand times a day, she'd think of something she wanted to tell Logan, or something happened she wanted to share with him, only to remember she couldn't talk to him. The nights were the worst, though.

She'd been making love with him every single night for the last fortnight—only to wake up and realize it had only been a dream. How long did heartache last? Shouldn't there be a freaking expiring date?

The front door opened and Lindsay stormed out, smiling broadly. "I thought you'd never get here! We had such a wonderful day!"

Charlie smiled and hugged her sister. She was so glad Gavin had agreed to join them. It was obvious Lindsay was happy and had, for a little while, at least, forgotten about nasty messages and phone calls and strange cars parked in their street. "What did you do?" she asked as they entered the house.

Gavin was lounging on the couch in the living room. "I would've been happy just drinking coffee all day, but Linds here had other plans."

"We went to the Chihuly Garden—Eleanor told us about it, remember? It's a showcase for the glass artist—"

"—Dale Chihuly." Charlie nodded. "Yes, I remember—it sounds fascinating."

"We have to come again when you won't have anything else to do—you'll love it," Lindsay said. "Then we went on a subterranean, walking history tour of the Pioneer Square—it was amazing!" Eyes sparkling, she described in detail the historic place they'd seen and how fascinating everything was.

Charlie caught Gavin's eye. They were both so pleased their sister was acting her old self.

"And where are we having dinner?" She smiled.

"Well, Brooke phoned. She wanted paintbrushes, which Gavin found, by the way, and she told me about this Italian restaurant they've been to when they last visited Seattle. Apparently, the food is out of this world."

"Sounds great. I just need a quick shower."

"How was your day?" Lindsay asked.

"Very nice, thanks. It was lovely to talk to other people who also speak Bowen." She grinned.

"You can tell us all about it. Go put on your glitters so that we can go."

Charlie's grin faded as she walked toward her room. She hadn't brought any of her usual tops on this trip. The reasons why, she didn't want to examine too closely at the moment. All she'd brought with her for dining out was a very sedate, very boring gray top to go with a pair of nice, if also boring, black pants.

CHAPTER 14

Halfway through dinner, Logan was ready to get up and leave. Why the hell had he thought taking another woman on a date would help him to not think about Charlie? Mandy was beautiful. The gray-and-white dress she was wearing was understated but obviously expensive. A pair of tiny pearl earrings was her only accessory. Stylish, neat, classic, she was the epitome of good taste. They'd been discussing several topics, all usually quite interesting to him. But he was so bored, he could weep in his wine.

Mandy hardly ate. The only thing she'd ordered was salad and even this seemed to be too much for her. She was explaining the new strategy she used for her more affluent clients, but he was struggling to concentrate. Thoughts of Charlie kept interfering.

Dating other women was not going to help him forget about Charlie—a fact that he'd have to acknowledge now, at least to himself.

A movement behind Mandy's head caught his attention. A waiter was showing three people to their table. He stared at them for a few minutes before it dawned on him they looked familiar. And it took his befuddled brain another few seconds to connect the dots: it was Charlie,

Lindsay, and her brother, if he wasn't mistaken. But it was a Charlie as he'd never seen her before.

Gone were the glittering top, the bangles, and the chandelier earrings. Her top was gray. Gray! And her earrings were almost invisible: a pair of pearl studs. Pearls, what the hell? Since when did she wear pearl studs? And her beautiful, long hair was gathered in a tight bun.

"Everything okay, Logan?" asked Mandy, and still stunned, he turned his head to look at his date.

"Logan, is there a problem?" she asked again with a tiny frown.

Finally, some emotion. He swallowed a sigh. Why was he here with this strange woman when he couldn't stop thinking about Charlie? "I'm sorry, I have to go," he said, and signaled to the waiter.

Fortunately, he'd met Mandy here at the restaurant, so he didn't have to take her home. He quickly paid the bill.

"Let me walk you to your car," he offered and took her arm.

No emotion, just a nod. Two weeks ago, before he'd met Charlie, he would've thought that this was exactly how he liked his dates to behave.

"I'm sorry, I shouldn't have…this…I…" But there really wasn't any explanation or excuse for his behavior. "My apologies. Where did you park?"

Charlie was laughing at something Gavin said when a movement made her turn her head and she saw the man she'd been dreaming about for fourteen miserable nights. She could only see his back, but that perfectly groomed, light brown hair, she'd recognize anywhere. Her heart skidded to a halt. A sleek brunette was walking next to him. They were leaving the restaurant, his hand protectively around the woman's elbow.

A sharp knife pierced her heart—the pain that followed, so intense, she nearly gasped out loud.

She tried to inhale fresh air, but a strap had tightened around her chest, making breathing difficult. Fortunately, Gavin and Lindsay were still laughing at the moment and weren't looking at her.

Of course, Logan would be dating other women; it shouldn't be such a shock to see him with someone else. But why, out of all the restaurants in a city the size of Seattle, would he'd be here, in this particular restaurant, tonight of all nights? It was so bizarre.

His date was gorgeous—thin, dressed in gray, not a hair out of place. Obviously, exactly the kind of woman he preferred. No wonder he'd told her she wasn't his type.

She looked down at herself and swallowed a sigh. Now she knew why she was dressed like this—without her beloved bangles, wearing gray. Gray. Seriously? She'd subconsciously tried to dress to please Logan. Even though she hadn't known she'd see him.

The waiter arrived with their wine, giving her a much-need moment to compose herself. She couldn't believe she'd forgotten all about her earlier resolve not to change for a man.

Smiling, Gavin raised his glass. "To us!"

"Good evening."

Charlie froze. She had to be daydreaming, or hallucinating. Logan had left the restaurant; it couldn't be him. Her head turned. But here he was, standing next to their table, with his eyes on her. In a black shirt and pants, he took her breath away.

Gavin's eyes narrowed. "What are you doing here, Johnson?"

"I can ask you the same question," Logan said, but he was looking at Charlie.

"I…" Oh, my goodness, what was up with her voice around this man? She cleared her throat. "I had a meeting. Here. In Seattle."

He held out his hand. "Can I talk to you?" he asked her. "Please?"

"Get the hell away from my sister," Gavin demanded.

But Logan didn't even look in his direction. "Charlie?"

"I don't think we have anything to talk about, do you?" she asked, taking a big gulp of her wine.

"It's been two damn weeks and I... Just five minutes, please?"

Gavin was getting up, his lips pressed tightly together. She knew that look. Before this spun out of control, she'd have to do something. Quickly, she put a hand on Gavin's arm. "It's okay. Just give me a minute."

Logan took her hand when she got up and pulled it through his arm. "Can we get a drink at the bar?"

Her heart was breaking into small pieces. "Logan, I don't know what you want..."

"I have to talk to you, damn it!"

The bar was adjacent to the restaurant, and from here, she could see Lindsay and Gavin. Her brother was standing, glaring in their direction.

"This will have to be quick—we've already ordered," she said when he pulled out one of the bar stools for her. Trying not to cry, not to shout out how she felt about him, left her swallowing furiously. Tiny strips of sticky tape were the only thing holding her tattered self together.

"What can I get you?"

She really didn't want another drink, but to get this over with as quickly as possible, she nodded.

"Dry white wine?" he asked.

"How do you know?" she asked, surprised.

His eyes darkened. "I know everything about you."

He ordered two glasses and took his seat. Their knees bumped and she moved sideways.

"Don't..." he said and took her hand.

"What do you want, Logan?"

His eyes were raking over her. "Why are you dressed like this?"

She crossed her arms. "Isn't this how you want the women in your life to dress?"

The barman put their drinks down, and Logan paid him without taking his eyes off of her.

"Gray is not you. Wearing damn pearl earrings isn't you. I..." He touched her face with his fingers. "I like the way you dress. I like your glittering tops, your soft, flimsy skirts, your bangles and I..." He touched her earlobes. "I dream about those mini-chandeliers you wear on your ears. Why the hell are you dressed like this?"

Damn it, those stupid tears were threatening to spill over; she had to put an end to this right away. She took a sip of the wine and tried to swallow down the lump in her throat.

"I'm trying my level best to get over you," she finally said, looking him straight in the eye.

His eyes darkened. "What if I don't want you to? I've missed you, damn it. I can't stop thinking about you and I can't work!"

She'd had enough. If she stayed here much longer, she was going to end doing something stupid like kissing him. Her whole being was urging her to walk into his arms. Quickly, she stood up. "Maybe if you replace 'I' every now and then with another pronoun, you'd understand you're breaking my heart. Please excuse me, my family is waiting for me." Quickly, she turned away and walked back to where Gavin and Lindsay were sitting.

"Do you want to leave?" asked Gavin when she reached their table again.

Exhaling slowly, she shook her head. "No, I'm fine." She looked up. Logan was still sitting where she'd left him, his gaze fixed on her.

What if I don't want you to? What did that even mean? She looked down at herself again. Logan was right about one thing, though—this wasn't her. She was done trying to please anybody else but herself.

Nothing she did, or didn't, do was going to help her forget about Logan. Nothing could. She loved him and that wasn't going to change. Ever. What she'd have to do was to learn to live without him.

"What did he want?" asked Lindsay.

"Nothing, really." She put a smile on her face and raised her glass. "Let's talk about something else, please. Here's to you, Gavin—may you join us sooner than later."

Her brother had finally stopped frowning, thank goodness. She forced herself not to look in Logan's direction again, but when they left at the end of their meal, she couldn't help herself. She searched for him.

But the chair at the bar where he'd sat was empty. Blinking furiously, she followed Lindsay and Gavin to their car.

He should've left after he'd put Mandy in her car. But no, he had to go back, had to try and get Charlie alone so that he could…what? Nothing about his actions after he'd seen Charlie tonight had been logical. But when he'd laid eyes on her, something else had taken over the reasonable workings of his mind.

Their short conversation kept playing over and over in his mind. She was trying to get over him. That's what she'd said. And that freaked him out, if he was honest. That was why he'd reacted with a stupid 'what if I don't want you to?'

She wasn't the kind of woman he could build a life with, damn it. He knew that. He'd told her she wasn't his type—something he struggled to remember when he was around her.

He wasn't even going to try to go to bed tonight. Sleeping wasn't possible. Not with his emotions all over the place, as they were at the moment. As they had been since he'd walked into Charlie's office. He made his living analyzing data, interpreting numbers, coming to conclusions about the figures so that he could find logical solutions to problems.

But how the hell did one analyze feelings? How were

you supposed to interpret wanting someone so much your whole body ached? And to what conclusion should he come when not a minute passed he wasn't thinking about Charlie?

If he couldn't use the basic tools of his trade, how did he find a damn solution to this craziness inside him?

Muttering and cursing, he poured himself a drink and pulled his laptop closer. There was so much work that needed to be done, he could do with an all-nighter.

But minutes later, he was staring out the window, his drink and computer forgotten. Charlie. She'd looked beautiful, but gray and pearls were way too mundane for her. No, Charlie was cascading hair, glittering tops, layered skirts, and bangles. Laughter and soft sighs, busy hands, and soft lips...

He rubbed his face, cussing a blue streak.

His phone rang. It was his sister. He quickly answered. At least if he talked to someone, he'd be forced to think about something else.

"Hi, Logan, I was thinking about you and wanted to check in—you okay?" Brooke asked.

He frowned. His mom and sister never just "checked in"—there was always a hidden reason for their call.

"Yes, I'm okay. Why?"

"No reason. So...uhm...how was your date?" Brooke asked.

And there it was. Of course, they would know. They made it their business to know about his comings and goings. "And how do you know about my date?"

"I...well...uhm, Mom told me."

"I didn't tell Mom."

"Well, it doesn't matter how I know about it, does it? The question is, did you enjoy it?"

And then the penny dropped. Usually he was quicker to connect the various dots when it came to his mom and sister, but he hadn't been himself for the past few weeks. But now he finally understood that finding Charlie and her family, in the exact restaurant where he'd taken his date to, hadn't been the bizarre coincidence he'd thought it was. His mom and sister had somehow orchestrated the whole thing.

"So, who spoke to Anna—you or Mom?"

Brooke laughed. "Oh, come on. You're not really mad, are you? We just thought maybe you could show Charlie and her family around Seattle, that's all."

Cussing, he got up and walked toward the big windows overlooking the city. "You do know the whole thing has nothing to do with you or with Mom?"

"I just can't believe she told you she loves you and you walked away."

"How the hell do you know that?"

"She told Mom."

"She told…?" *Well, hell.*

"Of course, Mom was upset when she heard you were on your way to Seattle instead of going to a cabin with Charlie as you'd planned. She went to see Charlie." Brooke sighed. "Charlie is one of a kind, and for a while, we really thought and hoped things could work out between the two of you, but if you're not into her, that's that. Anyway, tell me about your date. I really do want to know. My life is very boring."

"Yeah, right." He swallowed a sigh. "My date…well, she's beautiful. And nice."

"And?"

He rubbed his face. "And nothing. Good night, Brooke. Give Connor a hug from me."

"Logan?"

"Yeah?"

"Don't be mad at Mom—she wants to see you happy."

"I am happy, damn it!"

"It's just…life is so short, you know? I thought Adam and I had all the time in the world and then he was gone. Just like that. Don't wait too long. Take care."

Before he could respond, she'd ended the call. Logan

dropped his phone and started pacing.

He'd learned to keep a tight leash on his feelings and emotions ever since his dad had died. In his line of work, this had always worked to his advantage.

Giving in to feelings and emotions was messy, as he'd discovered since he'd laid eyes on Charlie. It distracted him from his work and made him miserable, and hell to live with, as Anna had pointed out several times. This madness had to stop right here.

Dating other women obviously wasn't going to help him get over this craziness, but he had more than enough work to keep himself occupied until these feelings and emotions had subsided.

But Brooke's words kept replaying over and over in his mind: life is so short.

CHAPTER 15

Monday morning arrived slightly cloudy. Gloomily, Charlie looked out of the window while she grabbed her bag from the table close by. They'd just finished breakfast and Lindsay was waiting for her downstairs. The day suited her mood and she hated feeling this way.

Ever since Logan had walked into her life, she'd been miserable. She'd known, right from the minute she'd seen his perfectly knotted tie, to be precise, she was not his type. Why then, did she fall for him anyway?

For the past week she'd felt tired, she was nauseous, she had no appetite, and after lunch she had a hard time keeping her eyes open.

Fed up with herself and her glum thoughts, she stomped down the stairs.

Lindsay raised her eyebrows. "Still in a mood, I see?"

Charlie immediately felt horrible. Ever since Lindsay had received the message from Mark, her sister had been on edge. At least Lindsay had a valid reason for not being herself. She, on the other hand, was wallowing in self-pity because she'd been so stupid as to fall in love with someone totally unsuitable.

She hugged Brooke. "I'm sorry. I've been a pain this

whole weekend. Please don't mind me. But I'm going to get over Logan Johnson, if it's the last damn thing I do."

"That's the Charlie I know." Lindsay laughed. "And I love the way you look, by the way."

Charlie threw her hair over her shoulder, jingled her bangles, and laughed. "This is me—weird and—"

"Wonderful." Lindsay interrupted her sternly.

"I don't know about that, but this is me. Anyway, I've always known I shouldn't fall in love."

Lindsay laid a hand on her arm. "If the right man comes along, he'll want you, not your womb," she said. "If he really loves you, he won't mind not having kids. At least, that's what I hear. I have yet to meet a man who isn't only interested in his own needs."

Gavin appeared from the kitchen. "What about me?"

"You don't count—you're family," Lindsay said. "And some woman will be very lucky to have you."

Gavin grimaced. "I've had it with relationships—way too much maintenance. I'm going for a run. See you later today?"

"Yes, shall we go to the bar?" Lindsay asked. "The usual crowd will probably all be there."

"It's Monday. Don't you have self-defense class late afternoon?" Gavin asked.

"Blake cancelled—he's apparently away for the rest of the month, maybe two, he said," said Lindsay. "So fortunately, I don't have to suffer through another session with him soon."

"I don't know why you're so irritated with him." Charlie giggled. "He knows what he's doing."

"That may be true, but he…I don't know, he just rubs me up the wrong way. Anyway, the cancelled class also means we can go out earlier!"

Gavin nodded. "Great. It will be nice to see your friends again."

Lindsay grabbed Charlie's arm. "Why don't we walk? It's cloudy but no rain is predicted and if it does decide to rain, Gavin can pick us up."

"Okay, maybe the exercise will be good for my mood." Charlie smiled.

Outside, Charlie locked the house while Gavin did some stretch exercises.

"Okay, I'm off!" Gavin called and with a wave, he started jogging in the opposite direction of where she and Lindsay were headed.

Lindsay quickly looked up and down the street. "Come on, grumpy, inhale some fresh air," she teased, and laughing, they started to cross the street.

They were in the middle of the street, Lindsay a step ahead of her, when the screeching sound of tires made both them turn their heads. A small, white car was coming toward them, fast.

For a moment Charlie was frozen on the spot. And then she realized—the car was going to hit Lindsay. Calling out, she dashed forward and pushed Lindsay out of the way.

Something struck Charlie against her side, hard. Swaying, she stared after the car as it sped away. Behind her, footsteps were approaching.

"Charlie! Linds!" It was Gavin.

Everything was going to be all right; Gavin was here. Maybe if she could just lie down for a minute...

By nine o'clock Monday morning, Logan had a splitting headache. When he'd arrived at six that morning, the headache was still faint, but over the past three hours, it had been getting worse and worse. It was probably because of his lack of sleep. He hadn't had a good night's sleep in...the hell if he knew.

His phone rang. It was his mother. He threw his phone in one of the drawers of his desk. This was one call he was going to ignore. The last thing he needed today was his mother nagging him about something.

Seconds later, the phone on his desk rang. It was Anna's extension. He grabbed the phone, while looking for pain tablets in his drawer. "What?"

"Your mother is on the line. She says you're not answering your phone and I know you're in your office." Anna quickly closed the door, and minutes later the phone on his desk rang.

"Damn it, I don't want to talk to my mother!" he answered the phone while rifling through his drawers. They were usually neat and tidy and he knew exactly where everything was—what the hell had happened here?

"Why?"

He sat back in his chair. Anna had put the phone through to his mother anyway.

"Hi, Mom. I'm…busy."

"Oh. Okay. I wanted to tell you about what happened this morning, but if you're too busy, I won't bother you." And before he could ask her what she was talking about, she'd ended the call.

Damn it to hell. He grabbed the phone again and dialed Anna's number. "Where the hell is the bottle with painkillers?"

She didn't answer him but hung up the phone noisily in his ear. He was still staring at the handset when she entered his office with a bottle of water in her hand. Without even looking at him, she marched toward his desk, opened the top drawer, and took out the bottle of pills. She put both the pills and the water in front of him.

"Thank you."

She marched back to his door and only when she'd opened it, did she turn back. "You are no fun to work for any longer. I'm leaving for the day."

"I'm sorry, Anna. It's just been…" He threw his hands up in the air.

"Your mother wanted to tell you what happened to Charlie this morning, but you didn't give her a chance."

A cold hand clamped around his throat. He got up.

"What happened to Charlie?"

Anna sniffed, turned around, and left, closing the door behind her.

Damn women. He patted his pockets. Where the hell was his phone? It took another few seconds before he remembered he'd put it in a drawer. *Charlie.*

What happened? And why couldn't his mother just tell him straight away? His fingers weren't very steady as he dialed his mother's phone number.

She answered on the third ring. "Yes?" she asked coolly.

"Charlie?" he got out, struggling to breathe.

"Minutes ago, you didn't want to talk to me," she said.

"Mom, please? What happened to Charlie?"

She sniffed. "We're all so upset, I wanted to let you know and then you were…"

"Mom!" he nearly yelled. "What happened?"

"Come to think of it, why would you be interested in anything that happened to Charlie? She told you she loved you and you left!"

"Mother, so help me…" He inhaled deeply, trying to stay calm. "What. Happened?"

"She was hit by a car. She and Lindsay were crossing the street…"

But Logan wasn't listening any longer. Charlie. Hit by a car. He had to get to her.

"I'll see you later, Mom," he said and ended the call.

Sheer terror threatened to cut off his oxygen intake, but he inhaled deeply and pulled his laptop closer. During a crisis, he was at his best. Usually. But the crisis had never been Charlie in an accident. His brain was sluggish, taking way too long to function properly.

What was he supposed to do? Plane ticket. Car. He had to get to Charlie. Nothing else mattered now.

Anna knocked and opened the door. "They're ready for you in the conference room."

Without taking his eyes off of the computer, he shook

his head. "Please shift the meeting to… Or better yet, ask Peter to take the lead on this one. I'll probably be gone for the rest of the week."

"You spoke to your mother?"

He nodded, searching for flights.

"Go and pack your things; I'll book the ticket and car and email the details to you," Anna said. "There's usually a flight just after one. I'll see if there is still a seat available on that one."

He looked up. Anna was actually smiling.

"What the hell is so funny?" Gnashing his teeth, he got up and grabbed his car keys.

"You, are, my dear." She chuckled. "You are."

But he didn't have time to wonder why Anna thought he was funny; he had to get to Charlie.

"Lindsay, relax." Charlie tried to calm down her sister. She was sitting on the bed in the doctor's rooms. "I am not going to the hospital, I'm totally fine. And what's more—the doctor agrees with me."

"You fainted!" Lindsay cried out. "Right there in the middle of the street. I've never seen you do that before."

"Well, I've never nearly been hit by a car before, either," Charlie muttered. The doctor had just left her to get dressed and had allowed Lindsay to join her. Charlie lifted her top to show Lindsay the bruise.

Lindsay inhaled sharply. "Just look at that!" she said, her eyes filling with tears. "I'll make you a mixture of myrrh, helichrysum, frankincense, and fractionated coconut oil, when we get to the shop. That should help with the bruising." She sniffed.

"It's not nearly as bad as it looks. I was probably hit by the side mirror of the car."

"You could've been killed." Lindsay sniffed. "We both could have been killed. Do you think it was him? Mark? I can't believe that freaking man is still out to ruin my life!"

"I didn't see the driver's face. Everything happened so fast. But he probably paid someone else to do this. He has the money to do that."

Charlie closed her eyes for a moment. The last hour had been a blur. Gavin had heard the noise and had rushed back, worried about them. He'd been in time to see the car speeding away, but he'd missed how Charlie had been hit.

He'd immediately phoned Eleanor, and she and Brooke had been kind enough to make arrangements for them to see the local doctor. Both Eleanor and Brooke had been waiting here at the doctor's rooms when they'd arrived. Brooke had also phoned the police; Gavin was probably talking to them at the moment.

"I hope the police can at least find out if he was behind this. But what did the doctor say about you?" Lindsay asked.

"I'm fine. The bruise will be sore for a few days, but it'll fade. He wanted to do all sorts of blood tests, as well, but I told him I'm fine, it's not necessary."

Lindsay frowned. "Blood tests? Why? Because you fainted?"

Charlie shrugged and straightened her top. "I don't know, but please stop worrying. I'm telling you, I'm fine. Let's go. Maybe the police can tell us something."

It was only when she took Lindsay's arm, she realized her sister was shivering badly. "Oh, Linds," she murmured, hugging her. "He is not going to get near you, I promise."

She took Lindsay's hands in hers. "Look at me?" She waited for Lindsay to look her in the eye. "Inhale, exhale. And repeat."

Within moments, Lindsay was calmer. "Thank you, sis. I'm just so upset that after all this time, he can still make me feel this way—useless and afraid."

"Well, you're not," Charlie said. "Come on, I want to get back to work if the police don't have any more questions. Thank goodness Lilly was able to move the appointments for this morning—I feel so bad about that.

Wouldn't you rather stay home with Gavin this afternoon? Lilly can look after the shop."

But Lindsay shook her head. "No, I'm fine. I have so much work—precisely what I need right now. Lilly, bless her heart, has been taking care of everything this morning."

The doctor stopped her before they left. "I really think we should run a few tests, though. People don't just faint for no reason. Whenever you feel up to it, just let me know."

"Thanks, Doctor, but I'm sure I'll be fine."

CHAPTER 16

By four o'clock, Charlie felt nauseous and her whole body ached. She tried to smile as she said goodbye to her last client, but she was so tired, she couldn't really care if she wasn't her usual pleasant self.

By the time she and Lindsay had arrived at work after lunch, everyone in the small town had heard about what had happened. Throughout the afternoon, people arrived with flowers, food, and all sorts of gifts. Even the mayor looked in to tell them he would make sure the perpetrator was caught.

She was so touched by everyone's concern, but with all the interruptions, her sessions took longer than usual. She'd asked Lilly to move the appointments for the last two people she was supposed to see to tomorrow. All she could think of now was to rest.

As she left, Lindsay looked out of her shop. "You okay? You look very pale."

"I'm fine, but I think I need to go and lie down. Gavin is picking me up. Will you be okay?"

"Of course. Lilly is still here. I'm just mixing another batch of the night cream, then I'll also be home. Shouldn't you go back to the doctor, Charlie? You're really very pale."

"No, don't worry about me. I just need a breather. It's been quite a day! I'll see you later. I'll ask Gavin to pick up something for dinner."

It was five o'clock in the afternoon when Logan reached Alisson. In the distance, the mountains rose high above the sky, usually a comforting presence, but today he barely noticed it.

He was frantic to see Charlie. He'd been trying to get hold of his mother and Brooke since before the flight, but they weren't answering their phones. So he still didn't know what had really happened. The only thing he was sure about was that Charlie had been in some kind of accident and he had to get to her as soon as possible.

During the nearly two-hour flight to Bozeman, images of everything that had happened between Charlie and him, had replayed over and over in his mind's eye. Charlie laughing, Charlie teasing him, Charlie with her arms around him, Charlie's face when they'd made love, Charlie telling him she loved him. Charlie telling him he'd hurt her.

And one searing question was driving him insane— what if Charlie was badly hurt or worse? What if…? He couldn't even think about it, let alone say the word.

Contemplating a world without her in it was inconceivable.

As he drove down the street in the direction of Charlie's house, he became aware of how tense he was. He wasn't even sure where she was, but hopefully someone at her house would know.

Her brother would probably try to throw him out, but even if he had to fight his way to get to her. He had to see Charlie today.

A commotion downstairs woke Charlie up. Combing

her hair back with her fingers, she sat up in her bed. What on earth...?

She could make out Gavin and Lindsay's voices but there was a third voice... Surely Mark Taylor wouldn't have the audacity to knock on her door, would he? She moved to get out of bed when her door flew open and in strode Logan. Her heart just about jumped out of her body.

Stunned, she stared at him. Logan was here. In her room. He looked different, somehow. What...? It took her a few moments to register what it was—his tie was hanging loosely around his neck and his hair was standing on end. The only time she'd seen him like that was...her heart sighed. Was when they'd made love.

"Logan..."

But before she could say anything else, a fuming Gavin appeared with Lindsay hot on his heels. "Who the hell do you think you are?" Gavin snarled, grabbing Logan's arm. "You cannot just storm into my sister's house and into her bedroom. You left, remember?"

Logan's eyes raked over her before he turned to Gavin and Lindsay. "I need a moment with Charlie, please?"

Gavin crossed his arms. "Anything you have to say to her, you can say in front of us."

Charlie got up quickly, but the whole room tilted. She quickly grabbed hold of the cupboard in front of her to steady herself.

"Look what you made her do!" Gavin bellowed.

"Gavin!" Charlie called out. "Please? Just... I'll be fine. I'll call you if I need you."

Gavin shoved his finger under Logan's nose. "You do anything to make her cry again, so help me—"

"Gavin, please?" Charlie tried again.

But Gavin wasn't finished yet. "You damn well—"

Lindsay fortunately stepped in and saved the moment. "Come on, Gav," Lindsay said softly, pulling their brother out of the room. "You're not helping." She gave Charlie a worried frown.

Charlie shook her head. "I'll be fine."

Still muttering and swearing, Gavin finally left with Lindsay.

With his eyes on her, Logan closed the door. "I'm sorry about that, but I…I simply had to see you. Are you okay?"

Afraid of keeling over if she took her hand away, Charlie leaned against the cupboard. "I'm okay. There really was no need for you…"

With two strides he reached her and the next moment she was pulled into a pair of strong, albeit slightly shaky, arms. "I lost twenty years of my life on the way to Alisson," he murmured in her hair, his hands stroking up and down her back. "If anything happened to you…" He pressed his face into her neck.

Her heart breaking, she clung to him. This was what she'd been longing for since the accident—for Logan's arms around her.

He was going to break your heart, Logic argued.

Oh, but think of the time you'd spend together, sighed Heart.

It wasn't really a battle; Heart easily won. Even if this wasn't going to last, she was going to enjoy these minutes with him. The heartache she'd handle when he left.

Her phone rang. She couldn't move, Logan was holding her so tightly.

"Logan?" She smiled against his chest. "My phone…"

Cursing, he dropped his hands and turned away while she answered her phone. It was Blake.

"Hi, Blake," she said.

Before Blake could answer, Logan had turned back, his eyes blazing. "What the hell does he want?" His eyes were mere slits, his hands on his hips.

"I just heard about the accident this morning," Blake was saying. "Lindsay isn't answering her phone. What happened?"

"I was just about to tell Logan about it…"

"Please tell me?" Blake interrupted.

Logan was shamelessly listening to her conversation with Blake and was getting more and more irritated by the minute. He grabbed her phone. "Listen, Davidson, I'm here, I will take care…"

He turned away and Blake obviously dropped his voice because Charlie could no longer hear what he was saying. Her head was pounding, she really didn't feel well, she wanted everyone gone. Rubbing her temple, she sat down on her bed again.

Her heart was still bouncing out of control. Logan was really here. In the flesh. Because he'd been worried about her. What did it mean? Did it mean anything?

Logan turned back. Much calmer, he returned her phone. "Blake is still on the line; he's worried about Lindsay. Will you please tell both of us what happened?" He sat down beside her and took her other hand in his.

The very last thing she wanted to do was to talk about this morning again. She was tired and scared and fed up with all these men who were suddenly interfering in her and Lindsay's life. But obviously, the only way she was going to get rid of both Blake and Logan was to tell them about the incident.

"Charlie?" Blake said in her ear. "Lindsay—is she okay? And you?"

"Lindsay is shaken, but she's fine. And I'm tired and irritated and really not in the mood to rehash the events of this morning, but I'm also okay. We are both livid that Mark was able to follow Lindsay to this little town. Whether it was him or whether he sent someone, is still unclear." Quickly she told them what had happened.

"So what did the police say?" Blake asked.

"Well, I haven't spoken to them again since this morning, but they were going to see if they could find any other witnesses."

"Are there any cameras in the area?" asked Blake.

"Not that I know of."

"Okay, thanks," Blake said. "Please tell Lindsay…never mind. I…I have to be here in New York for the next month, but please let me know if anything else happens?" He ended the call and Charlie put her phone down.

Logan was still holding her hand tightly, his eyes never leaving her face. "You're so pale," he muttered and combed her hair away from her face with his other hand.

"I'm really fine. You didn't have to come all this way…"

He frowned. "Of course I had to! All I knew was that you'd been in an accident. I didn't know whether you were hurt or…"

She pulled her hand out of his. "Why are you here, Logan?"

His eyes roamed over her face. "The last two weeks…" Inhaling shakily, he shook his head. "…were brutal. You're all I think about, Charlie. And I've missed you, I've missed us. I don't know what's going on inside of me, but I do know I want…I need to be with you." He grimaced. "And there I go again saying I, I, I—but that's how it is."

"I'm not sure what you're trying to say?"

"I'm saying I want to be with you. Whenever it's possible."

"For how long?"

"Until one of us wants…out."

She did her level best to paste another smile on her face. "A no-strings fling? Okay, yes, I can try that."

He frowned. "I don't know if I'd call it a fling. And the no-strings? I wouldn't want you… What I mean is, I won't be seeing anyone else while I'm with you."

If she had to look at him one second longer, she was going to burst into tears. "It's your choice." She forced a smile. "But now I need to lie down…"

He got up quickly. "Of course. Is there anything I can get you?"

"I'm fine. Please close the door on your way out." She got under the covers, thinking he was leaving, but he waited until she was lying down.

He bent down and kissed her forehead softly. Caring. Kind. He really was a good guy—that wasn't the problem. She kept her eyes closed, trying to keep the stupid tears at bay until he left. Only when she heard the door closing softly behind him did she turn on her side and let the tears fall.

Grabbing a tissue from the table next to the bed, she struggled to mop up her wet cheeks. Why was she crying, damn it?

A short fling with a very attractive man was really all she could ever hope for.

CHAPTER 17

Logan looked back over his shoulder toward Charlie's house as he drove away. She'd been glad to see him; she'd even agreed to his proposal to be with him whenever possible, so why was he feeling so disgruntled?

He should be thrilled. It was what he'd wanted. Wasn't it?

Minutes later, his thoughts still muddled, he parked in front of his mother's house. Even before his car stopped, the front door flew open and both his mom and sister rushed out.

"Logan!" his mother called out as he stepped out of the car, and she opened her arms. "I'm so glad you're here. Have you seen our Charlie? How is she? And Lindsay? We've phoned and Brooke took a pie over to their house earlier, but we didn't want to disturb them today."

"Mom." Brooke smiled. "Give the man a chance to catch his breath!"

Logan hugged his mom and sister. "They're both fine. Charlie is very pale, but she's resting now. I'll check up on her later tonight. Lindsay seems fine, too. Thanks for letting me know, Mom, and I'm sorry I was..."

"Rude?" his mom interrupted him.

He hugged her again. "Yes, I was rude. I'm sorry."

His mom patted his arm. "Of course, you're forgiven. Come on in."

"So, you're staying for a few days?" Brooke asked as they entered the house.

"Yes, probably until Sunday."

"Oh, I'm so glad!" His mom beamed. "So what does this mean? You and Charlie? Please tell me you've told her how you feel about her?"

"Well, we have an understanding. I'm going to try and get here as often as possible and she'll visit me in Seattle whenever she can." He smiled sheepishly. "Well, that's the plans I've made. I still have to run it by Charlie."

He was expecting them to smile and be happy for him; instead, his mom was frowning and Brooke was fuming. His sister was the first to speak.

"So what exactly have you told her?"

"That I've missed her and I want to be with her!" he called out, heartily fed up with these two women.

"And she agreed?" Brooke wanted to know.

"Well, yes."

His mother sighed. "My dear, sweet child. What did you feel when you heard Charlie had been in an accident?"

"I was in a state. Flying here, getting a car, and driving here, not knowing how she was—it nearly killed me. By the way, why weren't you answering your phones?"

"Because we were hoping you'd see what was really going on in your heart," Brooke called out. "But if even the thought of Charlie being hurt..." She rolled her eyes. "He's a hopeless case, Mom. Hopeless. We'll have to find Charlie another nice man to marry."

"She agreed to be with me. I don't know what you're going on about," he grumbled.

"She's told you she loves you and you're happy to have a fling with her!" Brooke scolded. She turned to their mother. "Ugh, I'll see you in an hour. I have to finish dinner. If I don't go now, I may just throttle your son."

Brooke wasn't really a much better cook than his mom, but looking at his sister's face, he should maybe just eat what was put in front of him without complaining tonight.

He picked up his bag. "I'll go change. And just for the record—I'm here." And without looking back, he took the stairs two at a time to the second floor. There were way too many women interfering in his life.

He and Charlie understood one another. He wasn't happy about calling what they would have a "fling," but did it really matter what it was called if he could be with her?

He put down his bag and walked toward the window. It wasn't difficult to figure out his mom and Brooke wanted him to marry Charlie.

Marriage? To Charlie? She was so different from him in every possible way.

Charlie was bangles and flimsy skirts and colored cushions and he was...? Well, he wasn't. Even the job she did was something outside the box. Deep in thought, he moved his body from side to side. But whatever Bowen therapy was, it worked. He'd been without back pain since the last time he'd been to see her in her office.

Besides, this feeling, whatever it was—lust, desire—it would pass. What Charlie made him feel, he'd never experienced before, but surely even these intense feelings couldn't last, could they?

Maybe after spending a week with Charlie, he'd feel differently. Which reminded him. He took out his phone. Depending on how Charlie felt, they could maybe finally spend a few days at a cabin, away from all the prying eyes of their separate families.

When Charlie entered the kitchen Tuesday morning, Gavin and Lindsay were already both having breakfast.

"Morning," she called out as gaily as she could. The last thing she wanted was for Lindsay to be worried about her.

"Oh, Charlie, you're still so pale!" Lindsay cried, grabbing Charlie's hands. "How are you feeling?"

"I'm…fine, I think." She pressed her hand against the bruise. "This is much better, thanks to your oils. I'm a bit nauseous, but maybe I'm just hungry. I slept right through dinner last night."

"Logan came to see you last night," Lindsay said.

"Insisted on going up to your room to make sure you're okay," Gavin grumbled.

"Well, you'll have to get used to him being around. At least for the time being," she said as she put two slices of bread in the toaster.

"What do you mean?"

"We're having a fling. For now. Neither of us wants anything more permanent, so calm down, Gavin," she hastened to add when her brother looked threatening.

"What the hell does that even mean?" Gavin asked.

"We'll be together when we can until…well, until he doesn't want to be with me any longer."

"And you're happy with that?" Gavin bellowed.

"I'm happy with that. Now please stop shouting, you're giving me a headache."

Gavin got up quickly and stormed out.

"You sure about this?" Lindsay asked. "Coffee?"

The toast popped out. "I'm sure. You know, I think I'll rather have tea."

"You, drink tea? Seriously, Charlie—are you sure you're okay? I don't think I've ever seen you drink tea in the morning before."

"I'm totally okay. Tea just sounds nice now." She turned around, looking for the tea. "Was Logan really in my room?"

"Gavin nearly had a fit, but he sidestepped him, bounced up the stairs, and sat with you for a while."

"Really?"

Lindsay nodded. "Really." She checked her watch. "And he should be here any minute now. I didn't tell him you'll be going back to work today."

Just then the doorbell rang.

"Let me get that before Gavin opens it," Charlie said and quickly rushed to the front door. Her stupid heart was already jumping up and down frantically, and she hadn't even seen Logan yet.

Logan had thought he was prepared to see Charlie again, but when the door opened and she stood there in a glittering, soft yellow top, gauzy, white skirt, mini-chandeliers dangling on her ears, he couldn't get a word out.

Smiling, she opened the door and stepped forward into his arms. For a moment she held on tightly to him before she dropped her arms again. But he wasn't nearly ready to let her go, so he cupped her face to keep her close.

"How are you feeling?" he asked. She was still too pale for his liking.

She pressed her face into his hand. "I am totally fine. I'm sorry I missed you last night, though."

"You were sleeping so peacefully I didn't want to wake you."

"Well, this morning I'm feeling much better. I have appointments this morning, though, but I can see you this afternoon?"

"I was hoping we could do that cabin trip we missed the previous time?"

She frowned, glancing over her shoulder. "I really want to, but after what happened yesterday, I don't want to leave Lindsay."

"But Gavin is still here," he tried.

"Yes, but he's in the process of moving here permanently and will be leaving soon to finalize his things in South Africa."

"What does he do?"

"He's part of a fund-managing group in Johannesburg.

He's hoping to continue working for them when he moves here."

"He and I should have a talk, if he's interested."

"Maybe not right now." She grinned. "He's very protective of Lindsay and me."

"That I can understand. So, no cabin then? May I take you to dinner tonight?"

Happy, she nodded. "That sounds lovely. You can also drop me off at work, if you don't mind?"

"Of course. What about Lindsay?"

"What about me?" Lindsay asked as she passed behind Charlie.

"He's offering to take us to work."

Lindsay widened her eyes. "Chivalrous, too. I like him, sis. A pity you can't keep him forever."

"Lindsay!" Charlie said, clearly embarrassed.

"What? If you were engaged, I could've said congratulations, but I'm not quite sure what to say when you are... How did you put it? Oh, yes, 'having a fling.'" She motioned the inverted commas with her hands.

Charlie laughed. "You don't have to say anything, Linds. Just be happy for us."

"If you say so. Just going up to get my bag!" she called out as she took the stairs two at a time.

"Me too." But before Charlie could move, Logan pulled her closer and kissed her. The moment his lips captured hers, everything around them faded away. This was home. Here with her. The smell of roses encircled him, and within seconds, he was ready to make her his.

Gulping in air, he lifted his head. "Woman, how the hell am I supposed to function today after that kiss?"

She blushed and turned away, dashing up the stairs. "I'll be back in a minute!" A glimpse of long, satiny legs nearly had him salivating.

Cursing, he walked back to his car.

"If you hurt her, you'll have me to answer to," Gavin snarled. He was standing next to Logan's car, his hands on his hips.

Of course, the brother. "Gavin. Good morning."

"There's nothing good about this morning. You're here."

"Well, get used to it," Logan replied.

Gavin's eyes narrowed, but before he could say anything, Logan took out one of his business cards.

"Heard you're thinking of moving here permanently. Give me a call; it sounds as if we could maybe work together."

Lindsay and Charlie were approaching, Logan opened the car doors for them.

"Why?" asked Gavin, waving the card in the air.

"Why not?" Logan swallowed his grin, for the first time not feeling defensive around Gavin.

Gavin didn't answer him, but he didn't throw away the card either. Progress? Maybe.

Charlie sat next to him as he drove them toward the small building where Lindsay's shop and Charlie's offices were. He took Charlie's hand. He simply had to touch her. Why was she still so pale?

"You feel okay?" he asked.

"She's still very pale, don't you agree?" Lindsay asked. "The doctor wanted to do some blood tests yesterday, but she refused. Maybe she'll listen to you."

He glanced at Charlie. "It couldn't hurt, could it?" He kissed her fingers. "Don't tell me a nurse is scared of a little needle?"

Charlie threw her hands in the air. "Okay, okay! I'll see if I can get an appointment with the doctor. Geez— Lindsay is bad enough—now I have to deal with you as well. I'm telling you, I'm fine."

He parked in front of the building and got out to open the door for the two women. Lindsay quickly said goodbye and walked toward her shop, but he couldn't let go of Charlie's hand just yet.

"What time can I pick you up?" he asked, playing with

her fingers.

"I'm not quite sure. But we can walk back home…"

Shuddering, he pulled her close. "Please don't. Promise me, until the police find out what happened yesterday, you won't walk anywhere? I'll talk to the sheriff again, as well. Maybe he can tell us what info the police have at this point."

"Okay, I'll promise. I'll let you know when we're ready to leave. But now I really have to go." She pulled out of his arms and with a wave, she walked toward her door.

Glumly, he got into his car. She didn't want to go away at the moment—he could understand that, but when the hell would he be able to be with her again? There always seemed to be people around them.

What he needed was a plan. A big part of his job was making new plans. Surely, he could find a way for Charlie and him to be together. And even before he'd finished the thought, he had a plan. Grinning, he sped back to his mom's place.

CHAPTER 18

Lilly popped her head around the corner at four o'clock. "So, what did the doctor say?"

"He's taken some blood and will let me know. But I'm really fine. I only went to the doctor to get Lindsay to stop worrying." She looked on her watch. "I've finished for the day, I think?"

Lilly shook her head. "Nope. You have one more client."

Charlie rubbed her temple and sighed. "Oh? Okay, thanks. I'm ready."

Lilly disappeared and Charlie inhaled deeply. She was tired, but it was a "good" tired. If she could just get rid of the nausea, she'd be back to normal. Probably still from yesterday's adrenaline surge.

There was a knock on her door. She looked up. Logan was closing and locking the door behind him. Her heart skidded to a halt.

"Logan?"

He began unbuttoning his shirt. "I've had to think of something to get you alone to myself," he began conversationally. "Then I remembered my back..." Purposefully, he walked toward her. "I think I'm in need of your hands on me." On his last word, his shirt was open and he was standing right in front of her.

"But Lindsay…"

"I've spoken to her. Gavin is picking her up," he said while his hands slid down her sides.

Oh, how she loved this man. But she swallowed the words and sighed. "Well then." Spreading her hands out over his torso, she smiled at him. "If that's what you need…" She bent her head so that her mouth could follow the movements of her hands.

But with a low moan, Logan gathered her in his arms and walked toward the narrow bed. "I've been dreaming about this damn uncomfortable table for two whole weeks," he said, putting her down on it. With unsteady fingers, he combed her hair back. "I have to see you…"

The playfulness was gone; in an instant her whole body was aflame, getting ready for him. She lifted her top over her head and with a quick movement, she removed her bra.

Eyes blazing, he covered her breasts with his hands. "Beautiful. You are so beautiful."

But then he noticed the bruise. His jaw tightened. "What the hell?"

"Probably the side window of the car."

With a soft curse he bent down and his lips softly caressed the injury. Her heart splintering into little pieces again, she breathed in his maleness, and her head fell backward. This moment would forever be a part of her; even when he left her, she wanted to remember every detail.

The sight of the bruise on Charlie's slim body made Logan see red for a moment. Who the hell would do such a thing? Gathering her close, his lips found hers. The kiss was meant to comfort, but her mouth was hot and eager, and within minutes his blood was roaring through his veins.

Making love to Charlie was like no experience he'd ever had. All his senses were heightened, each one absorbing as much of the woman with him as possible.

Spurred on by her soft whimpers, he slowly explored every inch of her body while feasting on her flesh. Satiny skin, soft curves, rose petals—all woman. All Charlie. He stroked and worshiped and caressed her until he was throbbing with need.

And when she trembled, calling out his name, he slid home. Enveloped by her velvety heat, watching her, he made sure she reached the peak first.

He tried to keep his eyes on her face, but his body had been without her for way too long and he let go. Spinning away with the sound of her cries ringing in his ears, he took them both to new heights.

At the precise moment her hoarse moan shot straight to his heart, the pieces of a messy puzzle finally fell into place. And for the first time he could see clearly—the reason he'd been acting like a lunatic was so simple—he loved Charlie.

For weeks now the chaos inside him had been trying to tell him that.

Of course, he loved her—he'd fallen for her the moment he'd seen her. His heart had known it way back then, but it had taken his freaking controlling mind a few extra weeks to catch up, damn it.

"Charlie?" he murmured against her ear.

"Mmm."

"I love you."

She stilled, stopped breathing. "You don't have to say that," she finally whispered, her arms still around his neck.

Frantic to make her realize he was serious, he loosened her arms and took her face in his hands. "You don't understand—I love you. I'm in love with you. What just happened between us? That wasn't just sex. That was me making love to you."

Blue eyes searched his face. "But you said…"

With a groan, he bent down and kissed her. "I said many stupid things. Please forget about all of it? I now understand why I've been so crazy over the last two weeks. I love you. Body, soul, and whatever else there may be."

And finally, blue eyes cleared. "You really love me?"

"I really love you. I can probably give you a few corny lines if that's what will convince you, but the bottom line is, I love you."

A slow smile lit up her beautiful face. "Give me one?"

But his fingers were tracing her collarbone, his body getting ready to devour her again. "One what?" he murmured as he bent down to kiss her shoulder.

"Corny line." She sighed and slid her fingers into his hair.

His lips followed the curve of her neck. "Really? You want corny lines?" He cupped her breasts; she trembled. "Okay, coming up, corny line number one—although this isn't really just a line, but true—you're my first thought in the morning and the last before I fall asleep," he whispered before his mouth closed around her breast.

With a soft sigh, she pulled him closer. "I love that."

But he didn't want to talk anymore. He wanted to show her how much he loved her—with his hands, his mouth, his body.

Charlie's phone rang as they drove away from her rooms. It was the doctor. She put her phone on silent. She was sure nothing was wrong, and if there was, she'd get whatever medicine she needed tomorrow.

At the moment, she was walking on air and felt absolutely fine. It was probably a combination of yesterday's incident, along with heartache, that had caused the nausea. Logan loved her. That was all she could think of right now.

He had her hand clasped tightly in his as he drove the

short distance to her house. They didn't talk until they turned off into the street where she lived.

"You okay?" he asked.

"I'm more than okay." She nodded happily. "You?"

"I'm a very happy man." He parked in front of her house. "I know we have to talk about all sorts of things…"

She bent forward and kissed him. "We don't have to figure out everything right now, do we?"

He pulled her closer. "I'd much rather kiss you than talk…" His lips welcomed her; she leaned in to the kiss.

She knew it was going to be near impossible to have a relationship given their circumstances, but she refused to think about that right now.

For the rest of this day, she was simply going to enjoy being with Logan.

"Mom!" Logan called out the moment he arrived back at his mother's house.

"In here!" she called from her studio.

She was standing behind a canvas on an easel, a paintbrush in her hand. As usual, the whole room was in total chaos. Her eyes lit up when she saw him. "You look very happy." Quickly she walked up to him and he kissed her cheek.

"I am. I've been with Charlie."

"Of course you have." Her eyes twinkled.

"I love her," he said, still stunned by the discovery.

She patted his arm. "That, I could've told you weeks ago."

"How? I only figured it out this afternoon."

"You men can be so slow sometimes. You couldn't see what Brooke and I saw. You never take your eyes off her, you know?"

"She's beautiful."

"Even if you don't like the way she dresses?"

Frowning, he stared at his mother. "Even if I don't

like…" he began slowly. He rubbed his neck. "But I love the way she dresses. I love everything about her. Why did it take me so long to figure it out?"

His mom's eyes teared up and she hugged him. "So what are you going to do about it?"

"What do you mean? We are…" What were they, exactly? Charlie had called it "a fling" but he now understood why he hadn't liked the word. The word *fling* implied something temporary and he didn't want temporary with Charlie. He wanted to be with her until his last breath.

How he could ever have thought what he felt for her would pass? Of course, he wanted her, but his feelings ran so much deeper. This was a forever kind of love. Forever. And that was what he wanted with Charlie.

"While you're figuring that out, come and look what I'm doing." And grabbing his arm, she dragged him closer to the painting she'd been working on.

He looked up and promptly lost his breath. It was a painting of Charlie in the off-the-shoulder top she'd worn the night they'd all had dinner together. With a few strokes of her brush, his mother had caught her essence—the gentle smile, those petal-soft shoulders and…

The lump in his throat was unexpected, he struggled to breathe. What his mother had also captured was the expression in Charlie's eyes. The same expression he'd seen when she'd told him she loved him, the same expression she'd had when they'd made love.

"When we all had dinner together, I took a photo of her with my cell phone," his mom said. "And I knew then I have to paint her. I wanted you to see what I see when I look at the two of you."

"She loves me," he muttered, staring at the portrait.

"Bless her heart, she does," his mother teased. "So, I'll ask again. What are you going to do about it?"

And then it was all so obvious. So clear. Stunned by the discovery, he stared at his mother. "I'm going to marry her, of course."

His mother burst out in tears. Alarmed, he hugged her. "Mom, I thought you'd be happy?" he said, stroking her hair.

"I am happy. So happy." She sniffed and patted her pockets. "I have to phone Brooke right away."

"Well, I'm taking Charlie out to dinner…"

"Are you going to propose?"

But he shook his head adamantly. "Of course not. I can't propose tonight; I need to put some thought into it, get the timing right. Besides, I don't have a ring…"

His mother's phone rang. She quickly glanced at it. "I have to take this, it's a client. But please remember, my dear child, you don't need a plan on a spreadsheet before you can ask Charlie to marry you. And there is your grandmother's ring, the one she left for you. You never wanted it before…" Turning her back on him, she answered her phone.

Slowly, he walked to his room. His dad's mother's ring. He vaguely recalled his mother talking about the ring, but he couldn't really remember what it looked like. Getting married was not something he ever thought would be part of his future plans. But that was before he'd met Charlie. Now everything had changed.

It wasn't as if he was going to use a spreadsheet… Or maybe it wasn't such a bad idea. Spreadsheets made things clear, brought order to chaos. His head racing, he took out his laptop.

Maybe he should return to Seattle before the weekend. He had a friend in the jewelry business; he could send him an email.

Half an hour later, he sat back in the chair. He'd accomplished what he'd set out to do. He had a plan, a plane ticket, and the promise of a ring. His mother could tease him all she wanted, but it was always a good idea to have a detailed plan.

This way, there were seldom surprises.

CHAPTER 19

"Anything else for you?" Logan asked as the waiter hovered next to their table.

Charlie shook her head. "Thank you, no. It was lovely."

While Logan asked for the bill, Charlie glanced at him. Something was wrong. He'd been strangely quiet all evening. After the waiter had shown them to their table, Logan had moved their chairs closer together, and all through dinner, he'd kept touching her, but he'd barely spoken a word to her all night.

For some or other reason, she'd hoped he would mention the future, even if it was only to say he wasn't sure how it would work. But although he'd been very attentive, he hadn't once referred to the afternoon they'd spent together.

But she shouldn't be disappointed. This was Logan, the man who'd told her that, in no uncertain terms, he wasn't in the market for a wife. What was more, she couldn't ever marry, she knew that.

For a few crazy hours, she'd let herself be swept away by the illusion that everything would be okay now that Logan loved her. But this was real life, and as she very well knew, things seldom worked out the way she'd wanted them to.

While they waited for the bill, he played with her fingers.

"Everything okay?" she finally asked.

"Of course. It's just...my plans have changed somewhat. I'm going back to Seattle tomorrow, but I'll be back this weekend. And I'd like to take you out to dinner on Friday?"

"Oh." Before she could say anything else, the waiter arrived with the bill, and Logan got up to pay him.

He helped her out of her chair and took her elbow as they walked toward his car. She loved the way he made her feel, but was this goodbye? What if he'd realized he didn't really love her, that he'd only said it in the heat of the moment, and to be honest—the moment had been seriously heated.

When he stopped in front of her house, she turned toward him. She had to swallow a few times before she could talk. "If you've changed your mind, please tell me? I don't want to wait until Friday to find out you've decided you've made a mistake—"

"What are you talking about?" he called out, pulling her close. "I love you. I've never told anyone that before and I mean it. But...I have... There are things I have to do."

He looked over her shoulder and grimaced. "And your brother is waiting for you on the porch." He quickly kissed her before he got out of the car.

While she waited for him to open her door, she breathed in and out. She wasn't going to fall apart because the evening hadn't gone as she'd dreamed. It wasn't as if she'd imagined him going down on one knee or anything, but a quick kiss and a "see you Friday" was not how she'd thought the evening would end.

Logan walked up the stairs with her to where a scowling Gavin was waiting. He ignored her brother and pulled her close for another kiss before he dropped his arms.

Then he lightly tapped Gavin on the shoulder. "You will have to get used to this. I love your sister." Grinning, he turned around and jogged back to his car.

Gavin's mouth was still hanging open as Logan sped away. "What did he mean by that?"

"Yes, whatever did he mean by that?" Lindsay asked, appearing behind Gavin in the doorway.

"The two of you weren't here when I returned from work this afternoon—" Charlie began.

"Maybe because you were so very late," Lindsay interrupted her with a smile.

"Otherwise, I would've told you. He says he loves me." She raised her hands. "And before you ask, that's all I know. He's leaving again for Seattle tomorrow. Apparently, he'll be back on Friday. I also don't know what that means."

Lindsay rushed forward and hugged her. "Of course, he loves you—it's so obvious, he can't keep his hands to himself around you. Oh, Charlie, I'm so happy for you! But why the frown?"

"It's just...this is all so new and now he's leaving again. I'm probably being silly. Anyway, enough about me. Have you heard from the police?" she asked, hoping to change the subject.

So many things had happened that day. She and Logan had made love; he'd told her he loved her, but even so, he was going back to Seattle. Initially, he'd said he was going to be here for the week, so why was he going back earlier?

Her head was struggling to keep up with her heart, and she needed some time to sort out her feelings.

Lindsay nodded. "Yes, Gavin and I went to see them this afternoon. They don't have much to report, though. Witnesses confirmed the incident with the white car in our street, but nobody can describe the driver. They couldn't find the car anywhere in our little town, so whoever it was has left already. Or he's lying in wait somewhere."

"Well, hopefully by now, most of the people in town

know about the white car and will be on the lookout," Charlie said.

Gavin closed the front door behind them and locked it. "I also think you two shouldn't go anywhere on your own until this whole thing has been resolved."

"I hate this," Lindsay said gloomily. "And there is nothing pointing to Mark anywhere although I know it's him."

"We can't do anything about it tonight, so go get a good night's sleep. I'll check all the windows downstairs," Gavin said. "And Charlie?"

"Yes?"

"You love this man?"

She nodded.

He placed an arm around her shoulders and gave her a quick hug. "Then I'm happy for you. But if—"

Charlie placed a hand on his mouth before he could complete his threat. "Relax, Gav, I'll be okay. I'm going to bed."

As she closed her bedroom door, her phone bleeped. A message from Logan. She quickly opened it.

I miss you

Sighing, she closed her eyes and pressed the phone against her body for a moment. He loved her. Whether that was going to change, she didn't know, but for now she was going to enjoy this giddy feeling. She quickly sent him a message, too.

Lindsay opened her bedroom door and peeped in. "Mmm, I knew you wouldn't be able to sleep."

Charlie patted the bed next to her. "Come on in. I've been so caught up with everything else, we haven't had a chance to talk today."

"You mean you've been caught up in all things Logan." Lindsay chuckled as she sat down next to Charlie.

"How are you?"

Lindsay sighed. "I'm so angry at Mark, but I'm fine. I'm just so sorry that my mess is now a problem for all of us."

"We're family." Charlie smiled. "So you haven't heard anything from him again?"

"No, but he obviously knows where I live." Shivering, she crossed her arms. "I was so stupid to fall for his charm."

"Don't you dare scold yourself. You walked away when you realized what he was like—that was very brave. And you're not the problem, he is."

"Uhm…Blake phoned just now. He makes me so mad…"

Charlie looked up quickly. "I'm glad you answered. He phoned me yesterday because you didn't take his calls."

Lindsay groaned, "I don't know why I have to talk to him! He's just another controlling man who feels he has to be in charge."

"You can't see Mark in every man. I haven't known Blake that long, but from what I've seen, he's one of the good guys. He seems to care about what happens to you."

"Well, I certainly don't need a man in my life," Lindsay said.

Charlie stared at her sister for a few minutes before she smiled. "You've got a thing for Blake!"

"Don't be silly. Of course, I don't have a 'thing' for Blake or any other man, for that matter. I don't know what gave you that idea."

Charlie pointed toward Lindsay's face. "Maybe the way you blush when you mention his name?"

"Don't be ridiculous," Lindsay said heatedly. "You're in love and now you're looking at the world through rose-tinted glasses."

A loud knock from downstairs stopped their bantering. Lindsay's eyes widened. Normally, no one went around knocking on doors this late.

"I'll go and look," Gavin called from the stairs.

Logan stared at his phone. Earlier, he couldn't wait to pick up Charlie for their dinner. But then she'd looked so beautiful, he'd struggled to string two sentences together. In a soft, blue glittering top that had dipped low in front, revealing a mere glimpse of the top curves of her breasts, she'd literally left him speechless.

And he couldn't tell her what was in his heart because, damn it, he didn't have the ring yet. He still needed to make plans. Charlie was special, so he'd have to come up with something exceptional when he proposed. Romance was not really his thing, but for Charlie he would try.

His phone beeped. Finally, a message from Charlie.

#cornyline2: You're in my inappropriate thoughts

And immediately, his body was ready for her. The little minx. He quickly phoned her.

"Hi," she answered, slightly breathless.

"So how am I supposed to sleep tonight knowing you have inappropriate thoughts about me?"

She laughed. "Good to know I won't be the only one struggling to sleep."

"I love you."

"Love you, too."

"See you Friday?"

"See you Friday."

After he'd ended the call, he kept looking at his phone. He should feel better, but he was still restless. Friday. Three whole days before he could see her again. Three whole days during which anything could happen.

"Knock, knock," his mother called.

"Come on in, Mom."

She had a small box in her hand. "This is your grandma's ring. I know you think you need to have a perfect plan before you can ask Charlie to marry you, but sweetie, you know, not everything in life needs to be strategized and prearranged. Sometimes, you simply have to listen to your heart." She put the box down next to him on the bed before she kissed his forehead. "You don't need a spreadsheet for love."

He picked up the small box as she left and opened it. For long minutes he stared at the ring. On top of a fine, gold band was a dainty cluster of diamonds and rubies—stunning, different, exquisite. Exactly like the woman he wanted to marry.

Without really thinking about it, he put the box in the pocket of his pants and walked out of his room. The light in his mother's room was on and he knocked on the door. "I'm going for a walk, Mom."

The door opened before he could turn away. His mom cocked her head. "Everything okay?"

"Yeah, I…I just need to clear my head."

She rolled her eyes. "Urgh! There's nothing to clear. You run a very successful business. And yes, you rely on your spreadsheets and on logic, but you also listen to your gut, don't you?"

"Yes, but…"

"That's what you have to do now, as well." Blowing him a kiss, she closed her door.

Deep in thought, he left the house and walked down the street where he'd played as a kid. It had been a great place to grow up in. Like their neighboring town, Livingstone, Alisson was surrounded by three mountain ranges—the Crazy, Absaroka, and Bridger mountains.

And rivers—closest to Alisson was the Alisson River, a branch of the Yellowstone River, where he and Brooke and their dad spent many summer days catching fish. An idyllic setting for a young boy. For all kids.

Kids. He'd never much thought about them. He loved his nephew, but would he even know how to be dad? His own had died when he so young, although he still remembered how Dad made everything better.

His thoughts flitted back and forth. But then he realized his Mom made everything better, too—even if it had been amid chaos. Chaos. For a moment he stood still before he resumed his walking.

For so long, he'd been so focused on what he'd experienced as chaos when growing up, he'd kind of forgotten what an amazing woman his mom actually was and what a big role she'd played in his life. Was still playing.

She'd raised two kids on her own while making every day fun for him and Brooke. Yes, his dad had been the steady one, but life without his mom would've been extremely dull.

For a while, he just walked, not really thinking about anything and when he looked up, he'd just turned off into the street where Charlie's house was.

But...a cold hand clutched his throat. Was that a police van? In front of Charlie's house? What the hell had happened?

He started jogging. Yes, the van was in front of Charlie's house and all the lights inside the house were on. With his heart in his throat, he ran closer.

CHAPTER 20

When they heard Gavin opening the front door, Lindsay jumped up. "Come on. I want to know what's going on. Fortunately, we're still dressed."

Both of them stopped at the top of the stairs. Two policemen were talking to Gavin.

Lindsay grabbed Charlie's arm. "Police? Why are they here?"

"Let's find out." They rushed down.

"They've apparently caught the guy in the white car," Gavin said.

Lindsay caught her breath. "Really?"

"Yes. We got a tip from Mr. Davidson—" the one policeman began, but Gavin interrupted him.

"Mr. Davidson?"

The policeman quickly glanced at his colleague, who was shaking his head. "Uhm...yes, Mr. Blake Davidson."

Lindsay inhaled sharply. "Blake? But what does he have to do with...?"

"We are not at liberty to discuss any further details," the other policeman said, giving his colleague a stern glance. "We're here to let you know that this guy is behind lock and key."

But Gavin still had questions. "So, this guy you've caught, what do you know about him? Is he from around here? Or…"

"I'm sorry, sir, we are not…" the policeman began, but before he could finish his sentence, the front door was pushed open.

Charlie blinked. It was Logan. But why?

He slapped the one policeman on the shoulder. "Come on, Harold, give these folks some info. Surely they have a right to know?"

His gaze found Charlie's and within seconds, he was at her side.

The policeman nodded. "He's South African. Ex-military. Entered the country about three weeks ago. He's all lawyered up and not talking. And that's all I can say. Good night."

"So, we still don't know whether…" Gavin began heatedly, but before he could finish his sentence, Lindsay's phone rang.

She quickly took it out of her jeans pocket, and scowled. "It's Blake."

"Well, answer it," Logan said. "Maybe he can tell us more."

Lindsay moved away and Gavin looked at Logan, scowling. "So, what the hell are you doing here again?"

Just then Lindsay returned, her lips pressed tightly together. "He wanted to know if I was fine, but he didn't want to answer any of my questions. Seriously, who made this guy king?"

"Well, from what I can gather, he's the one who was instrumental in making sure the guy who has been harassing you got caught," Gavin said.

"Nobody asked him to help," Lindsay grumbled.

Gavin looked at Logan. "Well, I would also like to know why strange men are suddenly interfering in my sisters' lives. Johnson, you haven't answered my question," Gavin said, crossing his arms.

"Gavin, seriously..." Charlie began, but Logan took her hand. There was a light in his eyes she'd never seen before.

"This was not the way I thought I'd do this, but my mom has assured me I don't need so many plans, so I'm going with my gut here."

Bewildered, Charlie stared at Logan as he patted his pockets. What was he going on about?

Logan took out a small, square box, the edges slightly frayed. He took Charlie's hand again. "The reason I wanted to go to Seattle tomorrow was to buy you a ring. Because you see, Charlie, I want you to know this thing we're doing here—I'm all in. I want to be with you until I stop breathing."

He grinned sheepishly. "I've made a spreadsheet of what I should do and when I should do it and how I should do it, but then tonight my mom gave me this ring—my grandma's—and I finally understood I don't need columns and plans."

He opened the box, but Charlie's gaze was fixed on his face. "I couldn't have chosen a more fitting ring if I'd tried. Exquisite, different..." His eyes were dark with emotion. "Unexpected, just like you. Charlie Wilson, will you"—he went down on one knee—"marry me, please?"

She hadn't known a heart could literally break, but in that moment it simply splintered into a million pieces. In front of her was everything she'd ever wanted but she couldn't say yes. It wouldn't be fair to Logan.

Shaking her head from side to side, she tried to talk, but her throat was clogged up. "I..." she finally got out, but then a sob from deep inside her prevented her from saying another word.

Logan frowned. "Charlie, sweetheart, I love you. I've been an ass tonight, I know, and I'm sorry but you looked so beautiful and I didn't know ..."

"You're everything I've ever dreamed about, but I can't marry you!" she cried out. "I've always had this picture in my head of a loving husband, a ranch, and a few kids but I...I can't have children and you'd be a wonderful father," she finally got out, tears streaming down her face. "There is nothing," she hiccupped, "I want more than to marry you, but I can't ever give you children."

Logan didn't miss a beat. "I'm asking you to marry me, not give me kids, Charlie. We'll make another plan if you really want children, but right now, my knee is hurting and I'm waiting for your answer."

She tried to wipe her cheeks. "Really?"

"Really. I love you, Charlie. You. I want to spend my life with you. Nothing else matters."

"Even though I'm not your type?"

He laughed. "You're not anybody's type. You're uniquely you. I love that about you. And I need that. I need you."

And finally, she could see in his eyes what her heart was still struggling to come to terms with—he really loved her. Her. The fact that she couldn't give him children didn't matter to him.

She fell forward into his arms. "Of course, I'll marry you," she got out before his lips found hers.

"Well, hell," Gavin mumbled, somewhere above their heads. "I think I've bought some bubbly. Come on, Linds, I'll get the glasses, phone Eleanor and Brooke. I don't think anybody's getting any sleep tonight."

They all ended up at Brooke's house because Connor had already been sleeping.

His mother had also arrived with a bottle of bubbly she "just happened to have" in her fridge, she'd said with a wink.

Logan couldn't stop grinning. He and Charlie were sitting on one of the couches, his arm tightly around her shoulders.

"Happy?" he asked Charlie, and she looked up at him.

Her eyes were glittering, her smile wide and carefree. "Very. What about you?"

"You're wearing my ring—I'm on top of the world." He picked up her hand. "I'm amazed that it fit. We can always change it, or if you'd rather have something more modern…"

She lifted her hand. "It's absolutely perfect. I love it."

"So," Brooke interrupted. "Tell us about your plans. When is the wedding? And what about after the wedding? Where will you live?"

Logan shrugged. "We don't have plans yet…"

His mother inhaled dramatically. Oh, no! My son doesn't have a plan? Whatever happened?"

Logan kissed Charlie's temple. "I met Charlie. She's home. Wherever she wants to live, that's where I'll be."

Clearly stunned, Charlie looked at him. "You can't be serious? Your work and life are in Seattle."

He shook his head. "My office is there, not my life. Today's technology makes it easy to work from anywhere. I meant what I've said—home is wherever you are. And as for the wedding," he said as got up, "will you excuse us for a while? I think my fiancée and I have things to talk about."

"We'll probably go home before you're back." Lindsay grinned. "Will you bring her home?"

"Of course. But it may not be tonight." He grabbed Charlie's hand and pulled her up. "I don't think I want to leave her ever again."

By the time they'd reached Logan's room in his mother's house, Charlie was breathless. Her head was spinning with everything that had happened over the past few hours.

The minute Logan closed the door, he pulled her into his arms and cupped her face. "I should be sorry I kind of ambushed you tonight when I proposed, but I'm not really. Are you okay with this?"

She nodded. "I am. But you do know we're very different, don't you? You're suits and ties and very tidy hair and I'm—"

"Glittering tops and bangles and dangling earrings, and I love it. I love you. Please don't ever wear gray again. You sparkle and glitter, sweetheart—that's part of why I fell in love with you."

The words were wonderful to hear, but she was still worried. "I'm not sure if you know exactly what you're getting yourself into. I'm going to have colored cushions and I'll probably mess up your home."

But he was still grinning. "I'm counting on it."

"Are you sure about…I can't have children?"

He kissed her face. "I love you and I want to spend the rest of my life with you. And if, at some point, you feel you want kids, we'll talk about it. There are various options, I believe. But whether you can have kids or not doesn't change the way I feel about you."

"If you're sure?"

"I'm sure. And as far as the wedding is concerned, I only have one stipulation."

"Yes?"

"I don't want to wait. I've waited my whole life for you. Now I want to be with you. Always."

She hadn't thought it was possible to be any happier than what she was, but she was discovering new depths of joy by the minute. Hugging him tightly, she rested her head against his chest. Below her ear, his heart was also racing at an alarming pace. "I'm happy with that. But I would like Gavin to be present, so we'll have to wait until he's back."

"Or," he said, lifting her chin with his finger, "we can get married before he leaves?"

She blinked. "I don't know if that's possible."

"Anything is possible if you put your mind to it. But can we talk about all of that tomorrow? Now I want to kiss my fiancée."

Grinning, she pulled his head down. "You do know I'm going to mess up your hair?"

"Looking forward to it," he murmured.

"Right answer," were the last words she got out before his lips captured hers.

And as a whirlwind of sensations lifted her off her feet, she held on tightly. Four weeks ago she hadn't even met Logan, and now she couldn't imagine a life without him.

It was still difficult to get her head around it, but it seemed he really loved her—glittering tops and colored cushions and barren womb included.

CHAPTER 21

Wednesday morning Charlie just made it to the bathroom before she was sick. By some miracle, she'd manage to keep her smile in place until after Logan had dropped her off at her house.

Minutes later, a worried Lindsay knocked and opened the door. "Charlie?" When she saw Charlie sitting in front of the toilet on her knees, she rushed in. "Sweetie, whatever is wrong?"

"I don't know," Charlie got out. "I'm so happy, but I feel absolutely miserable. Maybe it was something I ate…"

Lindsay brushed Charlie's hair back. "The doctor was looking for you yesterday. He even phoned me. Did you talk to him?"

Charlie nodded. "I got his message, but you know what yesterday was like."

Smiling, Lindsay sat down next to Charlie. "You got engaged! You're sure about this?"

"He loves me, Linds, and he wants to get married before Gavin leaves."

"Oh, my goodness!" Lindsay giggled. "The man is in a hurry, isn't he? Have you had time to talk about the future? You know—small details like where you'll live, and so on?"

Charlie shook her head. "Not really."

Grinning, Lindsay jumped up. "Well, first things first. Let's get you to the doctor. And we have to persuade Gavin to stay on for at least another month, although I'm not sure if one can organize a wedding in four weeks."

His mother and Brooke were in his mom's kitchen when Logan returned after dropping off Charlie. She had to work, he realized that, and what was more, he had a lot of work to do, as well, but he missed her already.

"Ah, the groom!" Brooke called out. "I am so happy for you!" She threw her arms around him. "Charlie is perfect for you."

"Thanks, sis. Yeah, she is. I'm a lucky man."

"So have you had time to talk about the when and where?" his mom asked.

"Not really. But she wants Gavin to be at the wedding and I'm not waiting until he returns—it could take months. So I'm hoping you guys will help so that we can do this before he goes back to South Africa."

Brooke was frowning. "What do you mean—until he returns? For another visit?"

"No, I assumed Charlie or Lindsay would've told you guys, but he's only going back to get his things in order. He's coming back to live here. Permanently."

Brooke's eyes widened. "Really?"

His mother was beaming. "Now isn't that good news? For the all the single girls in town, as well. He'll be kept very busy, I'm sure. So how much time do we have to plan the wedding?"

"Talk to Charlie. I'm happy with whatever you do as long as I don't have to wait more than a couple of weeks."

His mother already had her phone in her hand. "Let me phone her. A couple of weeks? I don't know if it's possible."

"Tell me what you need, I'll get it, do it, get someone to do it, but we're getting married as soon as possible," Logan insisted.

But his mother was already talking on the phone and she moved away.

Brooke cocked her head. "You look very happy"

"I am."

"You're really okay that she can't have kids?"

"You heard about that?"

"She'd told Mom a while ago, but Lindsay entertained us by enacting your whole will-you-marry-me performance of last night. I'm really impressed. I didn't think you had it in you to be so…so…spontaneous. And romantic!"

"See? I'm not always boring."

"Charlie brings out the best in you."

Just then his mom turned back. Frowning, she pointed toward her phone.

"Lindsay answered Charlie's phone. They're at the doctor's. Apparently, Charlie isn't feeling well. Didn't she say anything to you, Logan?"

Logan grabbed his keys again. "No, she didn't. She was very pale this morning and she didn't want coffee, but she said she felt fine. It's time she realized 'I love you' also means telling me when she's not feeling well. I'll phone you."

"Oh, he's got it bad," he heard his mother saying to Lindsay as he stormed off to his car.

Very true, he thought. Just the idea that something could be wrong with his Charlie had him feeling all tangled up. Why the hell hadn't she said anything?

Stunned, overwhelmed, choked up, Charlie walked out of the doctor's office. Lindsay got up when she saw her. Her sister still had the worried frown from earlier.

"What did the doctor say? You were awfully long in there."

"He says…"

But before Charlie could finish her sentence, the door of the waiting room burst open and Logan walked in. Troubled blue eyes immediately zoomed in on her. With two strides, he'd reached her side and pulled her close.

"Why the hell didn't you tell me you were feeling sick? What did the doctor say? Why didn't you phone me? What's wrong? I love you, damn it—that means you tell me everything."

By this time, all the emotion and tears that had been clogged up in her throat while she'd been listening to the doctor loosened, and a sob escaped. And grabbing hold of his shirt, she began to cry.

"Let's get her out of here," Logan said.

"Let me quickly pay the doctor," Lindsay said, nodding.

Logan put his arm tightly around Charlie's shoulders and led her out of the office.

Outside, Charlie tried to stop crying, but her body wasn't big enough for all the emotion and she needed a good cry.

Logan stroked her back. "Charlie, darling—please tell me what's wrong? What did the doctor say?"

Gulping in some fresh air, Charlie finally lifted her head and inhaled deeply before she tried to speak.

Lindsay exited the doctors rooms and rushed over to them. "Charlie—what happened?"

Charlie opened her mouth a few times before she was able to speak. In the next minute, she might not have a fiancé any longer. She had no idea how he was going to react when she told him the news.

"Charlie?" he asked again, cupping her chin.

"I'm…we're…pregnant," she finally got out. "I didn't know…" Still not quite believing it herself, she shook her head. "I was badly injured in an accident. Afterward, the doctors told me I'd never be able to have kids. I've made my peace with it. And then I met you. But then you said you don't mind and now I don't know if you'd even want a child. We haven't spoken about it. We haven't spoken about a lot of things…" Her words dried up.

"Whoop!" Lindsay cried and hugged her. "I'm so happy for you, but how is it possible?"

But Charlie's eyes never left Logan's face. All the emotion she'd experienced over the past half an hour, she could see in his eyes—shock, surprise, worry, and finally the one she'd been waiting for—wonder.

A broad smile lit up his whole face and he placed a big, warm, comforting hand on her belly. "A little Charlie with bangles and curls? I can't wait to see her."

Those stupid tears threatened to clog up her throat again. "It could be a boy who wants to wear ties."

The next minute, he picked her up in a bear hug. "I don't care. You're having my baby," he whispered in her ear. "Have you any idea how much I want you right now?"

But it was still difficult to believe that she could have everything she'd ever wanted. "So you're really okay with it?"

He placed her gently back on the ground. "I'm very okay with it." He checked his watch. "This calls for another celebration. How quickly can the two of you finish today?"

And while Logan and Lindsay made plans, Charlie leaned against her fiancé, drinking in his strength, his steadiness, his love.

It was still so difficult to get her head around it, but it would seem she was actually going to get her happy ending after all—the great guy, the kids and…

"I hope you like dogs," she interrupted him.

"Dogs? Uhm…do you want a dog?"

"Kids need dogs."

"Make that 'dog,' as in only one, and I'm in." Grinning, he bent down. "Told you I was all in," he whispered, then gave her a warm kiss. "The accident? Was it the same one in which your parents…?"

She nodded.

He pulled her close. "You've been through so much in your life. I promise you, I'll make it my life's mission to make sure you're happy."

"I'm happy with you." She smiled before he kissed her again.

His mom and Brooke were still sitting in his mom's kitchen when Logan walked in.

"How is Charlie? What did the doctor say?" Brooke asked.

His mom didn't say anything; she just stared at him. Before he could answer Brooke's questions, a broad smile lit up his mom's face and she held out her arms.

"Come and give Grandma a kiss. Charlie is pregnant, isn't she?"

"What?" Brooke shrieked and jumped up, hugging him. "But...how? And—I know this has nothing to do with me, but where? Haven't you always been surrounded by people?"

He bent down to kiss his mom. "A gentleman never tells."

"So I gather you're not mad anymore because I made an appointment for you with Charlie," his mom asked, her eyes twinkling.

He stared at her for a few seconds before he burst out laughing. "Aah, so you did set me up?"

Her smile was wide. "Of course. You were so wrapped up in your work, you couldn't see what kind of woman you needed."

"Am I glad Mom doesn't have a reason to interfere in my life again," said Brooke.

"Why do you say that?" his mom asked. "You're gorgeous. Any man would be lucky to have you."

Brooke sobered. "I've had my chance at happiness, Mom. It doesn't happen twice in a lifetime."

"We'll see," his mom said. "So, are we celebrating

tonight, I hope?" she asked Logan.

"Yes. Will you organize something for us, please, Mom?"

"Of course. Go play with your spreadsheets—Brooke and I got this."

In his room, he took out his laptop, but a few minutes later, he found himself staring at the screen, grinning like an idiot.

Getting married, having kids—he'd never really thought about it. But now he couldn't image his life any different. And at that moment, he knew exactly what he was going to do for Charlie.

Charlie closed the bedroom door behind them and turned into Logan's arms. "Thanks for this evening. I'm so glad we could share this with our families."

He led her to the bed. "You're not feeling sick at the moment?"

Smiling, she pulled him down next to her. "No, thank goodness. What I am feeling is happy. So very happy."

He brushed her hair back. "I've been thinking..."

"U-oh." Grinning, she began to unbutton his shirt.

He caught her hands. "If you do that, we won't be talking anytime soon."

She pulled her hands out of his and continued unbuttoning his shirt. "Don't you think we've done enough talking for one day?"

With a groan, he pulled his shirt over his head and caught her in his arms. "I love this about you," he murmured against her lips before her kissed her.

It was much later when Logan finally had the chance to tell Charlie what was in his heart.

"I want to start looking for a house for us here, in Alisson, as soon as possible. And I wanted to make sure—

will you be okay to leave your house?"

"Of course. I haven't spoken to Lindsay yet, but she can get someone to share the house with her. Maybe Gavin won't mind staying there until he's decided what he wants to do."

"I've asked him to join the firm," Logan said.

Her eyes widened. "Really? What did he say?"

"He hasn't said anything yet, but at least he's not glaring at me anymore," Logan said with a twinkle in his eye.

Charlie's smile slipped. "About the house—do you think we'll find something we both like?"

"Do you trust me?"

"Of course."

"The next few weeks are going to be crazy. You're going to have your hands full with organizing the wedding, and you're pregnant. Of course, I'll help you with whatever you want me to. Will you please let me find us a house and a venue for the wedding? But I'd like it to be a surprise for you. Will you trust me to get something that you'll like?"

Her eyes held his for a few moments before she let the sheet slip down. "I don't know. It will depend on your persuasion skills."

Grinning, he pulled her closer. "I'm told I'm very good at it."

"Well, then—show me."

CHAPTER 22

Charlie opened the window of her bedroom and sniffed in the fresh fall air. In the distance, against the backdrop of majestic mountains, the cottonwood forests were breathtaking in brilliant colors of orange and brown, and the cloudless sky was painted in indigo blue. This September morning couldn't be more perfect.

It had been the craziest five weeks of her life, but also the most exhilarating. Logan had been staying with her and Lindsay and Gavin over the last few weeks.

Exactly how their married life would work, she still wasn't sure. She didn't even know where they were going to live, but she also wasn't really bothered about it.

What she'd discovered about her fiancé over the past few weeks was that he knew exactly what she liked and that he'd move heaven and earth to try and find the perfect place for them. He got things done. They wouldn't have been able to pull off this wedding without his calm handling of every crisis.

The door to her room was flung open and she turned around.

"You're getting married today!" Lindsay announced, tray in hand.

Charlie hugged herself. "I'm getting married today. I still can't quite believe we've pulled this off! Organizing a wedding in five weeks? To be honest, there were times I rather wanted to elope."

Lindsay put the tray down before she sat on the bed. "Mostly thanks to your bridegroom, Eleanor, and Brooke. They were simply wonderful. Come and have coffee. Eleanor sent over some croissants with instructions for the bride to eat."

Charlie picked up a mug and warmed her hands around it.

"Isn't it the most glorious day?" Lindsay sighed as she picked up her mug. "It's chilly now, but the weather forecast is promising a mild and beautiful day. You feeling okay?"

"I'm great," Charlie said, putting a hand on her abdomen. "Thank goodness the morning sickness has passed."

Lindsay pointed toward her wedding outfit hanging against the cupboard. "I love your top and skirt; it's so you!"

"Logan was the one who insisted on a glittering top." Charlie giggled. "I was quite happy to go for something more classic, but he nearly had a fit when I mentioned it."

Lindsay sighs. "I love that he gets you. Are you in for a few surprises today—the man is pulling out all the stops for his bride."

"What do you know?" Charlie tried, but Lindsay blithely ignored her question by asking another one.

"So do you know where you're going for your honeymoon?"

"That's one thing I managed to figure out. I had a chance yesterday to sneak a peek at the plane tickets when Logan wasn't looking." Charlie giggled. "We're making a stop in Cape Town before we fly to the Seychelles. I had to know what to pack."

"That sounds fabulous! I'm so happy for you."

"You will look after yourself, though, while we're gone, please?" Charlie asked, and sat down next to Lindsay on the bed. "I'm so glad Gavin has agreed to stay until after we're back. And I'm very happy Blake is back, as well," she added slyly, waiting for her sister's response.

As Charlie had expected, Lindsay's lips thinned immediately.

Charlie grinned. "What is it with you and this guy? Everyone likes him but you."

"He's opinionated, irritating, and a know-it-all— everything I intensely dislike. You know why."

"Not all men are like Mark, you know."

The front doorbell rang and Lindsay jumped up. "I know, but Blake-freaking-Davidson makes me so mad. Don't worry, I'll be nice to him, seeing he's one of the groomsmen, though why Logan had to pick him, I have no idea. I'll go and see who's at the door. Gavin has already left; he's helping Logan with something. Eat up, the rest of the day is going to be crazy."

Charlie picked up a croissant as her phone bleeped. A message from Logan.

Can't wait to make you my wife later today

Smiling, she video-called him.

He was behind the wheel of his car.

"Hi, beautiful. Let me pull off the road. I was told I'm not supposed to see you."

"I'm sure this doesn't count. Where are you going?"

Smiling, he shook his head. "Still working on your surprises."

"I can't wait, but you're spoiling me."

"I love spoiling you. Did you get my present?"

"Another one? Logan, seriously..."

But before she could finish her sentence, Lindsay came bouncing in with a small package in her hands. "A present from the groom!" she sang.

With her hand on her heart, Charlie looked at her soon-to-be-husband on the small screen. "Hang on, here it is. Linds, hold the phone."

Lindsay took the phone while Charlie opened the small box. "Logan…" was all she got out. It was a pair of huge, golden hoop earrings with tiny diamonds all around. She picked one up. And then the tears simply refused to be held back any longer.

Logan frowned. "I can get you something else; just please don't cry!"

"She's crying because she's happy," Lindsay called out.

Sniffling, Charlie wiped her tears, and smiled at Logan on her phone. "I love it, it's perfect. You know me so well."

"I can't wait to see you." He blew her a kiss. "But now I have to go."

"We're getting married today. Surely you can tell me now where the venue is?" she asked again.

"Nice try, sweetheart, but it's part of your surprise."

He sent her a kiss before he ended the call.

Looking at Lindsay, she put the phone down. "And you're also still not talking?"

"Nope, my lips are sealed." Lindsay had another small box in her hand, which she gave to Charlie. "Your present from your bridegroom is probably your something new to show optimism for the future. I want to give you this for your 'something old.' According to Google, it stands for continuity, and the 'something blue' represents love and fidelity."

The tears were back and Charlie sniffled again. "Oh, my goodness, we have to stop crying before we do our makeup!" Charlie quickly opened the little box. It was one of the rings their mother had loved to wear—a fine, golden band with a blue stone.

With tears streaming down her face, she hugged her sister. "I was wondering what happened to this one. I looked through Mom's things the other day." She put on the ring. "Oh, Linds, you've had it re-sized—it fits! I had such a vivid dream of Mom last night."

Lindsay touched the ring, her eyes also bright with tears. "This way, she'll be with us all day."

The doorbell rang again.

"Eleanor and Brooke," they said together, and laughed through their tears.

As she and Lindsay ran down the stairs, Charlie wiped her tears. She wanted to savor every moment of this day. She was getting married to the love of her life.

Logan was watching the opening of the big marquee tent, when a waving hand caught his attention. It was Anna. She smiled broadly when he looked in her direction. Next to her were the rest of his team from work, who had all traveled to Alisson over the past few days.

Neither he nor Charlie wanted a big wedding and everyone who was there that day was someone close to them.

He returned his gaze to the opening of the tent. He couldn't wait to see Charlie again. Although it had been a very busy day, he'd missed her.

The past five weeks had been hectic. Fortunately, he'd discovered that Peter was very good at his job, and with Anna's help, things were running smoothly at the office. He'd probably go to Seattle several times a month for meetings, but he had no problem doing that as long as he could always return to Charlie.

She was in Alisson and that was home now.

"You nervous?" Blake asked.

Logan shook his head. "Just excited. Thanks for agreeing to stand here with me," he said.

"Of course," Blake said.

"Let me know when I can return the favor."

But Blake shook his head. "No, getting married is not for me. In my line of work—"

But there was a movement at the tent opening and Blake stopped talking.

The first one to enter was little Connor. He was carrying the small cushion with the rings and was clearly taking his responsibility seriously. He looked over his shoulder, and only started walking down the short aisle when Lindsay and Brooke, Charlie's two bridesmaids, also appeared.

The women looked beautiful, and Logan winked at his sister and new sister-in-law before quickly turning his gaze back to the opening of the tent.

The music changed and there she was. Glorious in a white, layered skirt and a shimmering pearl-white top that left her shoulders bare, was his bride. On her brother's arm.

His heart just about jumped out of his body. Her beautiful, long hair was hanging loose, the way he loved it, and she was wearing the earrings he'd sent her that morning. She nodded and smiled at the small group of people on either side of the aisle before she looked up at him.

Her whole face lit up, the way it always did when she saw him. His heart missed a beat. He adored the way she loved—openly, uninhibited, passionately.

Gavin shook his hand, hard, before he joined Blake.

Finally, he could touch her again.

"I've missed you, sweetheart." He took her hand.

"Missed you, too." She smiled up at him. "What is this place? It's beautiful," she whispered. "The homestead next door is absolutely lovely."

"I'm glad you like it—it's our new home. You did say you've always dreamed about living on a ranch."

Her eyes widened. "I can't believe you remembered that I said that!"

"I remember everything you've ever said," he said as they took their place in front of the altar. "Lots of space for all the kids."

"Then we'll have to get more than one dog."

"Of course."

"Sounds perfect." Her eyes shone even more brightly than before.

"Another thing—it's the ranch my dad owned."

Gasping softly, she hugged him. "I'm so glad for you."

The pastor cleared his throat and they turned toward him. Time to get married. To his Charlie.

It was very late when Logan finally carried Charlie into their new bedroom. He put her down slowly and she looked around her.

"Wow, it's so big!" she smiled.

"For all those kids we'll have."

But she was walking toward the big painting of herself his mom had done.

"Your mom?" she asked as he put his arms around her from behind.

"I wanted to buy it, but she nearly had a fit. Our wedding present, she says. You know what I saw the first time she showed me this?"

"How much I love you?"

"Exactly," he murmured as his mouth trailed a path down her face, over the satiny curve of her shoulder.

She lifted her hand and dragged his head lower. "And now I'm going to mess up your hair; you okay with that?" Grinning, she turned around in his arms.

"Counting on it."

And then no words were necessary. He was finally home. With Charlie.

ACKNOWLEDGEMENTS

Thanks to Melissa Keir and Inkspell Publishing for being a part of this journey – your support and encouragement mean so much to me.

I also have to thank the lovely Jeannie Steinman, also an author, who lives in Montana and was willing to share her knowledge of the beautiful state with me – I so appreciate your time and help.

Thanks to all the readers for your support and feedback – I couldn't have done this without any of you.

And as usual, a big thank you to my own real-life hero of 46 years, Theo, who cheers me on from the sides and who diligently reads all my words.

I hope you'll enjoy the journeys of the different characters as they find love in the fictional town of Alisson, Montana when they least expetect it.

Love
Elsa

SNEAK PEEK AT LOVE, IN WRITING

CHAPTER ONE

Margaret stepped into the elevator. Her shoes—with the ridiculously high heels that had looked so pretty in the store—felt like vices. She pulled the neckline of the tiny black dress to cover as much cleavage as possible, and groaned. It didn't help; there simply wasn't enough material.

Praying no one else would want to use the elevator, she pushed the button on the panel. Enough people had seen her near-naked state as it was. Another punch at the button indicated Margaret's tide of frustration boiling up inside. Why wouldn't the doors close?

Perhaps going home was the best idea after all. She didn't have to stay in her brother Josh's flat. Her own comfortable bed in Kommetjie wasn't that much farther from Sea Point. Only round the mountain, really. Yesterday, when her brother suggested she spend the night in the guestroom, it sounded like a logical way to avoid driving the extra fifty kilometers. At the time it seemed like a good idea, but after this disastrous evening, she only wanted to get home.

Why couldn't she stand up to her family? *A vicars-and-tarts party*. She shuddered. Trust her cousin Louise, who was turning thirty, to pick such a theme for her birthday party. She should have refused to go. She had hoped a night out would stop her worrying about the financial state of her bookshop for a few hours, but Louise's catty remarks about how she was wasting her inheritance only made her feel worse.

And of course, she should have refused Josh's offer to stay over at his place in Sea Point. But mostly, for once in her life, she should have had the guts to stand up to Louise the minute her cousin had begun to coax her into changing her demure vicar's costume for this scrap of fabric.

And then Louise had insisted she meet a good friend of hers. Margaret rested her head against the mirror in the elevator and closed her eyes. The good friend's eyes had never even met hers. His gaze had been glued to her cleavage the whole time. She'd finally managed to escape the octopus-like arms of Tim or Tom or whatever the man's name was. It took time and the last shreds of her patience to convince him no, she wasn't playing hard to get, she really, truly wasn't interested in a roll in the sack, as he'd so movingly put it.

The doors finally closed. She opened her eyes, only to stare straight into a pair of gorgeous, pale blue ones. An incredibly attractive man lounged against the wall of the elevator, arms folded, his insolent stare raking her from head to toe. Where had he come from?

Her first instinct was to try and cover up her cleavage, but she wouldn't give him the satisfaction. She lifted her chin. Surely the elevator should have stopped by now?

"You'll be the second one tonight," he said quietly, and smiled.

Stupefied, she looked at him. "I beg your pardon? Second one?"

Unhurriedly, he stepped closer to her. She was in the corner of the elevator and couldn't move.

"There was also one in the restaurant where I was trying to have my dinner. Who told you about my apartment? How did you know I'd be here? Who are you?"

He stood awfully close to her making it hard to breathe properly. Tall, tanned, short, light brown hair. The bottom half of his face stubble-covered, making him look very sexy.

His lips were moving, spewing out a barrage of

questions but she couldn't make sense of what he was saying. The doors closed and the elevator started to move.

"Um…I'm sorry, what?"

He was now standing so close to her she was forced to tip her head back. He reached out a hand and caressed her cheek, kindling embers smoldering just beneath her skin.

"Look, you're pretty enough and I really wouldn't mind taking you up to my flat. Just tell me how you knew where I lived. You won't be the first girl to stalk me and you probably won't be the last, either. But tell me. How. Did. You. Know?"

Margaret gaped. His mouth was moving but it took a few minutes for her befuddled brain to process what he was saying. She was fascinated by his face, the movement of his lips, the taut skin of his cheeks. Her eyes couldn't move away from him. He was really beautiful. What was he saying? Gradually, his questions penetrated her brain.

"What… Who are you? You must be mistaken. I was at a par—"

He nodded and put his hands into his pockets. "Is this how you're going to play it? You're going to pretend you don't know who I am?" He was smiling, but it wasn't a nice smile.

She had no idea what the man was talking about. All she knew was she had to get out of the elevator, and fast.

Margaret swallowed and shook her head. Breathing had become so difficult and for a minute, she worried she might faint. He was standing right in front of the door and she started to squeeze past him so she could get out as soon as the elevator stopped. He turned with her, his eyes never leaving hers.

"Like I said, I don't mind taking you up to my flat…" His voice dropped to a whisper. "You really do have the most amazing eyes."

He walked closer, and she stepped back. And still he moved closer. She tried to step farther back, but was blocked by the side panel behind her. Their faces were so close together, she could see the tiny flecks in his eyes. His musky male scent seeped through her entire being. She swallowed. Althouhg he was scowling, she didn't feel threatened. His gaze dropped and a hiss escaped through his teeth.

Margaret looked down. The top of her lacy, red bra was clearly visible from this angle. Her eyes gaze flew back to his.

Leisurely, his gaze connected with hers again. The sudden flash of desire in his eyes robbed her of the last of her breath. As if in a trance, he lifted his hand and tucked a lock of hair behind her ear. With a look of fierce concentration, he trailed his fingers down her cheek.

His eyes darkened; he cupped her face in his hand. Around them, the air sizzled with strange electricity. He had the palest of blue eyes. A sound penetrated her befuddled brain. Oh, my goodness, it had come from her throat. His eyes mirrored the confusion she was experiencing. Then, as if stung, he dropped his hand and stepped back.

"But not tonight, okay? I'm too tired," he said in a clipped voice. The elevator stopped, the doors opened, and he quickly disappeared.

The doors closed again. Oxygen, she needed oxygen. Margaret gulped in some air and sagged against the wall. What on earth had happened here? Who was this man? What did he think she wanted? Too many questions to process at this time of night. She looked down at her hands. They were trembling. She had almost allowed him to kiss her. Even worse, she had nearly taken the initiative and kissed him. She had to get home quickly. Her heart was racing; her palms were sweaty. Why would she be in such a panic? Yes, the man was attractive, but she'd never reacted like this to other attractive men. He had completely mesmerized her.

When the elevator stopped on the floor where Josh had his flat, she stared at the empty corridor for a minute then pressed the button to go down again. She'd finally made up her mind. After what had nearly happened, she was not staying in this building another second. She pressed her hand against her heart. It seemed to be settling down. Finally.

On the way down, the elevator stopped on the second floor. The doors opened. The man she'd seen before stepped in and stopped in his tracks. Her heart began its crazy galloping again. The doors closed behind him and the elevator moved.

"So you're still around? Well, darling, if you really want to, I'm happy to oblige but I need to get something from my car."

Her eyes grew huge.

He smiled at her. "You really are persistent, aren't you?"

What was he talking about? She tried to speak, but her mind was a complete blank. Meeting drop-dead gorgeous men in elevators was so *not* part of her boring life.

It was crazy to react in this way. What was wrong with her? And then it struck her. Of course. This was "The Face" she'd been looking for. She'd been trying to find a face for the hero in her latest romance novel for over a month now. She'd browsed through magazines, searched the internet, tried to pick out that one striking face in a crowd, one who would be her hero's, but it had never been the right one.

And there he was. She'd found him. Tonight of all nights, when she hadn't even been looking, she found him.

***

A hardcore Science Fiction writer and a softhearted romance novelist clash on the sunny South African coast... Margaret Parker is a hopeless romantic whose fantasies fuel her writing. For Graham Connelly, science fiction is the perfect genre to express his cynical worldview. A chance meeting in a lift leaves them both interested and aroused — with no clue as to the other's identity.

Margaret has been looking for a face to match her new fictional hero — and Graham's is it. Graham has been looking for proof that innocence and optimism still exist — and he's found it in Margaret. But fantasy isn't reality, and both Margaret and Graham are used to controlling their fictional worlds. Can they step off the pages long enough to find their own happy-ever-after?

She writes romance. He science fiction.
A relationship seems unlikely, can love find a way?

Available Where Books Are Sold...

ABOUT THE AUTHOR

Elsa has been reading love stories for as long as she can remember and when she 'met' the classic authors like Jane Austen, Elizabeth Gaskell, Henry James The Brontë sisters, etc. during her English Honours studies, she was hooked for life.

She married her college boyfriend and soul mate and after 46 years, 3 interesting and wonderful children and 4 beautiful grandchildren, they are now fortunate to live in the picturesque little seaside village of Betty's Bay, South Africa.

She likes the heroines in her stories to be beautiful, feisty, independent and headstrong. And the heroes must be strong but possess a generous amount of sensitivity. They are of course, also gorgeous! Her stories typically incorporate the family background of the characters to better understand where they come from and who they are when we meet them in the story.

Webpage: www.elsawinckler.com
Personal Facebook page:
https://www.facebook.com/elsa.winckler
Author Facebook page:
https://www.facebook.com/ElsaWincklerRomanceAuthor?ref_type=bookmark
Twitter: https://twitter.com/elsawinckler @elsawinckler
Goodreads:
https://www.goodreads.com/author/show/6557709.Elsa_Winckler
Pinterest: http://www.pinterest.com/elsawinckler/
Wattpad: http://www.wattpad.com/user/elsaw1
Instagram: https://www.instagram.com/elsaw1/